THESE HAUNTED HILLS

A COLLECTION OF SHORT STORIES
BOOK 4

Jan-Carol
Publishing, Inc

"every story needs a book"

These Haunted Hills
A Collection of Short Stories
Book 4
Published September 2022
Mountain Girl Press
Imprint of Jan-Carol Publishing, Inc.
Copyright © 2022 Jan-Carol Publishing, Inc.

ISBN: 978-1-954978-62-1
Library of Congress Control Number: 2022946014

You may contact the publisher:
Jan-Carol Publishing, Inc.
PO Box 701
Johnson City, TN 37605
publisher@jancarolpublishing.com
www.jancarolpublishing.com

This is dedicated to all the talented authors for their participation in this collection of short stories, and to all the readers of Jan-Carol Publishing's books.

TABLE OF CONTENTS

THE MAN IN THE FOG

JEFF GEIGER JR.

My mom picked me up from school on the day I turned sixteen, and she drove me straight to the DMV in Johnson City. She knew how badly I wanted to get behind the wheel; I pestered her and my father all the time about it.

After I passed my driving test, Mom let me drive her car home. As I pulled onto the main road, I glanced over to see her gripping the car's grab handle like it owed her money.

"You okay, Mom?" I asked, even though I could tell she was nervous.

"Yes, honey," she said, taking a deep breath. "Just keep your eyes on the road."

I did, but I didn't stop with the questions.

"How am I doing?"

"Fine," she said. "Just fine."

"So," I began. "You think I can drive myself to practice tonight?"

I felt her eyes on me when she said, "I don't know if that's a good idea, Jake."

"I'll be fine, Mom. The baseball field is only a few miles from the house."

"I'll have to discuss it with your father."

I knew what that meant. It was Mom's way of putting a conversation on hold.

When I pulled Mom's car into the driveway, I noticed my dad's truck sitting there next to another vehicle. Dad walked out of the garage just as I put the car in park. After I opened the car door, I heard him ask, "What do you think, Jake?"

I got out and hurried over to the car, looking at it in awe. "Whose car is this?"

Dad tossed the keys, and I caught them in my hands.

"Looks like you'll be able drive yourself to practice tonight," he said with a grin.

I shifted my gaze from the car over to my mother. It must have been the smile across my face that helped her make the decision. "Just be careful, Jake. Text me when you get there and before you leave."

"I will, Mom," I said, hugging her. "I promise."

I kept my promise too. I made it to the field safely that night and sent her a text message saying so.

While I was grabbing my baseball bag out of the trunk, Vic, the best guy on our team, walked up to me.

"Nice ride, Jake."

"Just got it today."

"Like it?"

"Love it."

"That's good, man," Vic said, his eyes shifting to the ground.

"Yeah," I said, studying his face. "What's going on? You okay?"

"You haven't heard yet, have you?"

"No, should I have?"

"Owen," he said as he crossed his arms. "He went missing last night after practice."

"No way."

"His parents were a little late to pick him up yesterday. It was dark out, and Owen wasn't anywhere to be found."

"I hope he's okay," I said, closing the trunk and slinging my bag over my shoulder. "I'm sure his parents are worried."

"Of course they are," our coach said from behind us. "Hustle to the field. And don't worry, guys, I'm sure they'll find Owen."

"Let's hope so," Vic said, then he took off toward the field.

A couple of hours later, practice was coming to an end. The sun had just set, and coach was finishing up his after-practice pep talk for the big game this coming weekend.

As our team walked off the field, everyone headed to the parking lot except for me. After the gallon of water I drank during practice, I desperately needed to use the restroom.

By the time I made it out to the parking lot, everyone had left. My car was just where I had parked it, facing the woods. The headlights and taillights flashed a few times when I pressed the unlock button on the key fob. I tossed my bag in the trunk and slid in behind the wheel.

Before I started the car, I remembered that I needed to text my mom to let her know I was leaving the field. I got out to retrieve my phone from my baseball bag, which was still in the trunk, but before I got the trunk lid to open, I heard someone call my name.

"Hello?" I said as I spun around.

The voice sounded familiar, but it was too far away to make out.

Weird, I thought, looking toward the woods. Then when I turned back to face the car, I saw him. He was still wearing his practice clothes from the night before.

"Owen, what the hell, man! Don't you know everyone is looking for you?"

"Yeah, I know," he replied with a quick nod.

"Come on, hop in. I'll give you a ride home."

"I can't."

"What do you mean, you can't?"

He looked to his left and right. "I have to show you something first."

"Show me what? I have to get home or else my mom is going to have a conniption."

"Please," Owen said, his eyes narrowing on mine. "You have to see it to believe it."

His jaw was set, his arms hung loosely by his sides, and he looked sick. I mean really sick.

"Okay," I said. "But let's make this quick."

Owen nodded and began walking toward the woods. I followed

him, wondering what it was that he wanted to show me.

"I don't know about this, Owen."

He spun around. His eyes took on a feral look for a second. I had known Owen since the fourth grade. We had been good buds over the years; he even stayed the night at my house a few times. In all those years, though, I had never seen him look at me the way he was looking at me now.

"Now, Jake. Before it gets dark."

I'm not sure why I followed him. As strange as I'm sure it sounds, it was as if he was moving my legs *for* me.

"Where are you taking me?" I asked him as we entered the woods.

"Have you ever been back here before?"

"No, I've never had a reason. These woods always kind of freaked me out."

"Well, yesterday was the first time I had ever ventured out here."

"And?"

Owen stopped. His eyes became large and round.

"What's—"

"Shhh," he said. "Just be quiet."

I felt my arms break out in gooseflesh. "I'm going back."

"No," he said, his lips quivering. "You have to see this."

"Why me?" I asked.

"Because you're the fastest one on the team. It has to be you."

"I don't understand."

"You will," he said, letting out a sigh. "We're getting close."

A few minutes later, I noticed the sun had set completely. I was still able to see, but it was only getting darker. Owen took a sharp left and continued to walk. It felt like we had walked a hundred yards when we finally reached what he wanted to show me.

Trees surrounded where we stood, but just forty or fifty feet in front of us was fog. It seemed to go on for miles, but there was really no way to tell.

"This is crazy," I said. "How'd you find this?"

He faced me and said, "Listen to exactly what I say when we go in there."

"Why would we go in there?" I asked, becoming annoyed.

"Because," he said, as fresh tears trickled down his cheeks. "That's where my body is."

* * *

I was struggling to process what Owen had just told me. Finally, I said, "If this is a joke, it isn't funny."

Owen wasn't smiling. Not even a little. "I told you that you'd have to see it to believe it, didn't I?"

"But—"

"It's in the fog, behind a redbud tree. The only way I can rest is if you carry it out of the fog for me."

If he was acting, his performance deserved an Academy Award. "You swear this isn't some practical joke?"

Owen took a deep breath, wiped away the tears, and raised his hand toward me. "Shake my hand."

I looked at him as if he was crazy. At this point, I had been pretty sure he was until I went to grip his hand. My hand passed right through his. I stood their looking at Owen's hand as it went through mine, feeling nauseated for a few seconds. When it passed, I looked up and saw the dejected look on his face.

"All you have to do," he said, pointing at the fog, "is go in there and carry my body back to the parking lot. Call the cops and tell them what happened."

"Owen," I said. "What exactly did happen?"

"There's a man in the fog. I'm not sure what he is, but I know he only wants to hurt people."

"Is he the one that," I paused, searching for the right words, "did this to you?"

Owen nodded.

"What if he kills me, Owen? What then? Did you ever think of that?"

"He won't."

"How can you be so sure?"

"Because I've learned that he can only see you when you move. If you're perfectly still when he looks in your direction, you won't be seen."

"How do you know that?"

5

"The girl in the fog told me. I tried it too. It works. Trust me."

My legs started moving, but I swear I wasn't the one doing it. I was walking toward the fog, Owen just a step or two in front of me.

"Remember," he said. "Do exactly as I tell you."

"Okay."

"And if he looks our way, don't move a muscle. I mean it."

I nodded.

For the life of me, I can't tell you why I went into the fog with Owen that day. Maybe he had some hypnotic power over me. Or maybe it didn't take much persuasion since I really did want to help him.

When we entered the fog, the air around us seemed to drop twenty degrees. The fog was so thick that I had a difficult time seeing just five feet in front of me.

"Don't worry," Owen told me. "It isn't this bad up ahead.

"Are we almost to the tree?"

"Keep your voice down," he said, looking to the left and right. "It's probably another two hundred feet or so."

"When does the fog become less—"

The fog thinned out before I could say, 'intense.'

Owen's right hand shot out, his palm toward me. His left pointed ahead of us.

Several children were running around in the fog, playing tag.

"Those kids' bodies never made it out of the fog. The girl," he said, moving his pointer finger to the left. "She's the one who told me I had to get someone to move my body out of the fog if I didn't want to be trapped here. She's also the one who told me the man can't see us if we stay still."

"And you believe her?"

"The man didn't see me earlier today. He looked right at me, but I didn't move at all. Then he just kept walking until he disappeared into the fog."

"How do you know she's right about removing your body from the fog?"

Owen bit his lower lip as he lowered his head. When he looked up, he froze. "Don't move," he said, not moving his lips.

I stared ahead, not moving. My heart began to pound against my ribcage when I saw him.

He was walking toward us. A dark silhouette of a large man with glowing red eyes. As he continued to walk in our direction, I closed my eyes, fighting the urge to turn around and run away. I was the fastest kid on the team, but something told me that the man in the fog would be faster, or that I wouldn't be able to find my way back.

When I opened my eyes, the man was gone. I didn't move, though. Not until Owen said I could.

"Okay," he said after a minute or so. "He's gone for now."

I let out a deep breath, shaking as I exhaled. I looked down and noticed that my fists were clenched tight.

"Take it easy, Jake. You're okay."

"Let's get your body and get the hell out of here."

Owen nodded and started walking.

Kids ran in front and behind us. Some skipped, their arms swinging by their sides. *How long have these kids been stuck here*, I thought as I followed Owen through the fog. Soon we came upon the redbud tree. The one he said his body was next to.

Owen said, "Don't freak out when you see it, okay?"

I nodded and followed him to the other side of the tree.

There in the grass, the fog floated slowly over Owen's dead body. I felt my eyes well with tears involuntarily. Owen's neck was severely bruised and twisted in a way a person's neck should never be twisted. The rest of his skin had turned a bluish gray. And I noticed something else: the body seemed to be sinking into the ground as if it were slowly trying to bury itself.

"It's sunken even more," Owen said, his hand over his mouth. "It wasn't this far down in the dirt earlier."

I didn't want to touch Owen's corpse, much less carry it, but I did what simply had to be done. I slung Owen's lifeless body over my shoulder. The stench of his corpse nearly knocked me over. I began to feel nauseated again like I had earlier, but this time it was far worse.

I said, "Let's go, Owen. I want out of here now."

When I didn't get a response, I looked around.

"Owen," I said again.

"Over here."

I could barely see him in the fog, but I started walking toward his voice. As I got closer I could see him perhaps twenty feet ahead of me. Then I saw a flash of something grab Owen and pin him to the ground. It made a laughing sound similar to the laugh a hyena makes when feeding on its prey.

His glowing red eyes looked in my direction.

I forgot to stay still.

The man in the fog held Owen by the throat. I feared for him even though he was already dead. What snapped me out of it was when Owen managed to shout, "Run, Jake! It's too late to be still. He's seen you!"

I turned around, looking for a place to hide. Up ahead I saw the girl that Owen pointed out earlier.

"Over there," she said.

I narrowed my eyes in the direction she was pointing. It's the way Owen was headed before the man in the fog attacked him. I followed her index finger above the trees to the faint glow of the parking lot's light poles.

I knew which way to go now, but I had a one-hundred-and-fifty-pound corpse over my shoulder, and the man was standing in the way of me escaping.

He was holding Owen down with his foot now, staring at me with his arms spread out as if to say, *Where do you think you're going?*

I turned around, even though it was the wrong way, and began to run.

As soon as I did, the girl stopped me. "Go," she said, pointing where the man had been.

"This is your only chance."

"But the man," I said, stopping mid-sentence when I saw what she was pointing at. The kids that were playing tag and skipping along in the fog earlier were all over the man. I saw Owen there on top of him, one arm around his neck while the other covered his glowing red eyes.

I lunged forward, running through the fog, trying my best not to trip. My best wasn't good enough, though. I was maybe eighty feet ahead of the man when I stepped in a hole and tumbled over. My head hit the ground hard. Owen's corpse slammed against the ground next to me. I looked up at the night sky, blinking several times until I could see straight again. My head was pounding when I sat up, looking around for the man in the fog. When I didn't see him, I got to my knees and worked on getting Owen's body over my shoulder again.

Then I heard Owen scream.

I lifted his corpse over my shoulder and saw the man in the fog sprinting in my direction.

Before I could even turn around to run, he was right in front of me. He shoved me hard, and I fell back down. This time I didn't hit my head, but Owen's corpse landed on top of me. A second later I felt the weight of his body sliding off me. The man was pulling the corpse by the legs. I felt something round and hard by my right hand; it was a rock about the size of a baseball. I quickly threw it at the man's head. It connected with one of his glowing red eyes, and he dropped Owen's body. He wasn't done, though.

I looked around for something else to defend myself with and didn't see anything at first.

Then I found a broken branch from a black oak tree on the ground, roughly the size and shape of a baseball bat. I spun around and saw the man dragging Owen's body back into the fog. I got the broken branch and ran up behind him. When he turned to look at me, I swung as hard as I could.

His head made an unpleasant cracking sound when the branch connected. He fell down hard, releasing Owen's body as he descended. I lifted Owen's corpse over my shoulder, for what I hoped would be the last time, and ran for my life.

A short while later the fog began to thicken, just as it did when we first entered, which meant I was close to getting out of this nightmare. It seemed too good to be true. I just knew at any moment a hand would reach out and snatch me up my ankle, or that I'd trip again and not be so lucky this time around.

But none of that happened. One second, I was running through the fog and the next I was out of it, breathing hard while I tried to remember how to get back to the parking lot.

I soon found the path and jogged down it with Owen's body still over my shoulder. The stench was still there, but it either wasn't as bad

9

now, or I was just getting used to it. Or maybe I didn't care anymore because I could see a glimpse of the parking lot. As I kept jogging, I saw something else too: red-and-blue lights.

Two squad cars were parked next to mine. To the right of those was another car: my mom's. I was sure my parents had called the police when they got here to find my car without me anywhere near it.

Even though I had just rescued my friend's corpse from some sort of supernatural creature in the fog, I was still scared of what was to come of this.

"There he is!" I heard one of the police officers say as he shined his flashlight on me.

The doors to my mom's car flew open, and I saw my parents running toward me just behind the two police officers.

Before they could get to me, my legs gave out and I collapsed just outside of the woods.

The police officers looked down at Owen's corpse. "Is that the kid that went missing yesterday?" one of them asked.

I didn't know if he was asking me or his partner, but I said, "Yes. It's Owen."

"How'd you find him?"

Now I knew he was talking to me. "He told me to go in the woods. He said I'd have to see it to—"

That was when my mom shoved past them and wrapped me tight in her arms. My dad was there next to her. They were as shaken up as I was—probably more.

Mom and Dad helped me to the backseat of the car. My legs still felt like gelatin, but I had helped my friend the only way I could. I couldn't bring Owen back, but at least he wasn't trapped in the fog anymore.

Then I heard one of the police officers say, "Hey! Where'd the body go?"

"What do you mean?" His partner yelled. "It's not like it could just walk off!"

I shifted my gaze toward the woods.

They didn't see them, but I did.

Through the trees, in the darkness which lies behind them, were two glowing red eyes floating deeper and deeper into the woods.

THE HOUSE BREATHES

BEV FREEMAN

("The House Breathes" is the third installment of "The House" published in *These Haunted Hills: a Collection of Short Stories Book 2*)

Winter came on with brute force in East Tennessee's mountains. Breanna's Weather Alert sounded on her phone, waking her at 5:00 AM with one eye open she stared at the message. Snow Warning for NW NC and NE TN: accumulations possible 8–10" by 7:00 AM.

Breanna sat straight up in bed and texted to her BFF, Lauren. No school today! Bundle up and meet me by the creek @ 6:30. She and Lauren had a chosen meeting place along the creek dividing their subdivision from the open land of the National Forest.

Lauren's reply chimed in, It's dark out.

Yea, and cold, still snowing, too. Be sure to wear your high top boots! Breanna touched send as her bare feet sunk into the fluffy rug next to her bed. She pulled her flannel-lined jeans from a shelf in her closet, the snow pants next to them, and the fur-lined waterproof boots. After putting on a long sleeved tee shirt and brushing her teeth she put her auburn hair into a high ponytail. She scribbled a note to her mom saying she'd be out with Lauren until about noon.

Tiptoeing to the kitchen, she placed the note next to the coffee pot.

She checked to see what time the Auto-brew was set. *Seven, that's good.*

After putting on her favorite hoody and water resistant jacket, she rushed out into the winter wonderland. Streetlights illuminated blanketed shapes, offering no hint of what lay beneath. Breanna made her way to the end of the street locating the path draped by overhanging evergreens. She entered a tunnel only winter can create and waited by the half frozen stream.

Lauren joined her by the creek's edge, "Isn't it a beautiful snow? I followed your tracks. Otherwise I might have missed the path; everything looks totally different!" She sipped a steaming liquid from her Yeti.

"Where's mine?"

"You don't even drink coffee." Lauren attempted an apology.

Breanna laughed, "Just kidding. Yea, it is so nice before anyone else steps all over the lovely ground cover. This way we can track a deer or maybe a fox. I love this wilderness scene."

"Me, too. As long as it isn't a wild hog or a bear track we find!" Lauren looked up and down the creek bank. "It doesn't look as though anyone is out but us."

Shallow as the creek was, most of the water tumbled through rocky outcroppings of large stones. Deeper, slow moving pools supported a layer of fresh snow and suggested a layer of ice beneath. The girls moved upstream toward the forest, watching closely for any disturbances or tracks.

"Bree, look. There's a tiny track, what is it?"

"A weasel, I think. But where'd it go?" Breanna bent at the waist to observe the track.

"There." Lauren grabbed Breanna's arm. "You almost stepped on it."

"Oh, gosh, I'm glad you saw it." She focused her attention. "Mr. Weasel, you're stunning in your winter coat. We didn't mean to disturb you." She fished her phone out of her coat pocket and took a picture.

"I've never seen a white weasel. It sure is pretty."

Breanna answered, "They're like some rabbits that turn white in winter so they'll blend into the snow."

They both watched the little critter for a few minutes and then it darted up the hill leaving a faint trail. After a couple steps they heard a loud crack in the underbrush.

"The weight of the snow might break down some branches. We should watch out." Breanna snapped her head toward another sound. As she turned toward the action, a large buck jumped the creek nearly running into Lauren.

"Did you see the rack on that guy?" Lauren lunged to the side just in time. The buck ran like his life depended on it. And maybe it did.

"Are you okay?" Breanna grabbed for her friend offering her hand to help Lauren out of a snow drift. "That looked like at least an 8 pointer." With the other hand she pointed her phone camera toward the deer trudging through deep snow.

Another crash sounded even closer; or felt closer was more like it. Among the underbrush on the opposite bank, a cloud of white billowed into the air and then settled quietly around a towering black form.

Standing like a granite statue staring at the girls, the hulking creature uttered a low growl. Moving only their eyes, Lauren and Breanna glanced at each other and returned to watching in disbelief. They, too, were frozen in place.

Snow continued falling, covering the top of the head of whatever stood in front of them. "Back up slowly, don't run. Don't take your eyes off it." Lauren softly whispered.

Being careful not to step off their own footprints the girls retreated far enough that the creature elected to step across the frozen creek. Running up the steep hillside as if it were level ground, the creature continued pursuing the buck. Two frightened and bewildered teenage humans ran as if their own lives depended on it—in the opposite direction.

"We are okay, aren't we?" Breanna asked. "How did you know to walk away like that anyhow?" She breathed a sigh of relief. "Let's get out of here now."

"Don't you watch the *Bigfoot Chronicles*?" Lauren chose her footing as she waded through a shallow part of the creek.

"Oh, I wasn't aware they'd declared an actual Bigfoot Protocol." Breanna answered, following closely behind her friend. After a while

Lauren stopped, bent to catch her breath and then burst out in laughter. "Did you take a picture? I bet it's blurry."

"What?" Breanna shouted. "Look at me. My hands are shaking. My heart is pounding out of my chest. Are you kidding me?" Breanna still held tightly to her phone.

"You put it on video when the buck tore up the hill." Reaching for the phone, Lauren pulled it away to search for any sign of a photo or video.

"I don't know if it was running or not. I was too scared to think about it!"

Lauren tilted her head to one side. "That's funny. The video of the deer is perfect. The last crash recorded, but only the sound. Bree, it doesn't make any sense."

"Oh, no, let me see." She snatched her phone. "How did this happen? Looks like some kind of interference."

"Isn't that the way it always happens? Photos of Bigfoot are either blurred or messed up some other way. This should have been a good video."

As the two walked they realized they were by the plantation pecan trees. "Look, there's the old house. Let's see if Samuel is here. I wonder if he's seen the Bigfoot fellow." Breanna darted to the back door of the kitchen.

Samuel happened to be looking out the kitchen window. "Come on in."

Breanna opened the door, slipping out of her boots before stepping inside the newly remodeled, updated kitchen. "Hey, glad you're here. Have we got a story for you!"

"Come in, come in, I'll fix you some hot cocoa. It's cold out there this morning. Aren't you gals freezing?" He turned to the new eight burner gas range and lifted a tea kettle off a low flame. "Always good to keep some hot water going. Don't you think?" He then reached into the cabinet taking out a box of Nesquik Chocolate Mix. "I make my own. It's better than store bought."

"I agree," Lauren perched on a high kitchen chair and pulled up to the matching high table. "I like your new kitchen. You have good taste, Samuel."

"Why thank you, Lauren. I had some help." He snickered but didn't explain. "Now tell me about your adventure." He poured the mugs half full of mix and stirred while he added hot water.

"You might not believe us, but we encountered, um..." she looked to Breanna for help. "A large creature, not a bear..."

"You mean you met Mr. Bigfoot?" Samuel set the mugs on the tall table in front of his guests. "I've seen him too. Not really a friendly feller, but he don't bother me and I don't bother him."

Breanna swallowed a hot gulp of cocoa. "You've seen it?"

"Sure, he's been here, well forever. I came across some old letters out in one of the slave quarters. They talked about him way back a hundred years ago and more."

"Slaves wrote letters?" Lauren questioned. "Was there a name signed to them?"

"Yeah, can't remember what it was though. I've got them upstairs." Samuel sat in one of the chairs and continued drinking his cold cup of coffee. "My coffee never stays hot long enough for me to drink it." He stood and walked to the new microwave oven, setting the mug inside.

"You need a Yeti cup, like mine." Lauren pulled the empty cup from her backpack. "It keeps it hot or at least warm, all day, and in summer ice stays frozen all day."

"That's what the Yeti is for? I have one upstairs. Guess I'll bring it down and try that." Samuel took his hot mug back to the table.

Breanna forgot all about Mr. Bigfoot after Samuel mentioned the slave letters. "I don't want you to have to run upstairs right now, but sometime I'd love to see the letters. If you don't mind, that is."

Samuel nodded his head and then sipped his coffee. "Let me see your video, will ya?"

Breanna pulled it up on her phone and showed him the photo of the little white weasel and then the video of the buck. They listened to the loud crash where the picture fuzzed off the screen. "We felt the noise more than just hearing it. It jarred the ground. Snow shook off trees and all the underbrush. And then when the cloud settled, there he stood." She shuddered as she thought about what they witnessed.

"That's the buck I missed at the end of hunting season. He sports a twelve point rack! I might get him if Bigfoot didn't catch him today."

Leaning back in his chair, Samuel rubbed his chin with thumb and forefinger. "Yeah, you definitely saw Mr. Bigfoot. Nothing else out there is big as him. Must be eight feet or more, don't you agree? The way he steps over the creek—" Samuel breathed deeply, pressed his lips tight together, and shook his head side to side slowly.

"I told Mom I'd be home around noon. We better hit the trail, Bree." Lauren stood, picked up both their mugs and carried them to the sink. "Thanks for the chocolate. I really needed that."

"Yes, and it's nice of you to warm us up." Breanna walked to the door and slipped into her boots. "Say hi to Mr. Bigfoot next time you run across him."

The girls walked the path alongside the familiar wrap around porch. When they reached the door to the cellar, they stopped. On the ground in front of the door were a couple of large, barefoot prints leading away from the house.

Breanna moved closer and looked down onto the steps. "You don't think—" She looked at Lauren. "Na, that can't be."

The girls walked at a quick pace away from the yard of the plantation house. Reaching the creek crossing, they were thankful the area was frozen over solid enough to hold their weight. Memories of the bridge collapsing gave Breanna a chill. She sure didn't want to fall in the freezing cold water. And the bridge had not yet been rebuilt.

Deep snow crunched under their boots when they walked on the road. But that was not the only sound they heard. Away in the distance, deep in the forest, something made a loud crack. It sounded like a wooden baseball bat struck against a strong tree. Momentarily two more cracks rang out.

"Tree knocks, it's what Bigfoot Researchers call that sound. They say if you answer it, you're signaling or communicating with the Sasquatch." Lauren slung her backpack over her shoulders and started running.

Breanna followed her lead without question. The two did not stop before reaching the street of their subdivision. Understanding an oath of silence, the girls parted.

"Call me later?" Lauren shouted at Breanna who was already half a block away.

"You bet!" Breanna waved and continued walking toward home and the safety of her loving family.

No one is ever going to believe our story. Not even if we say Samuel has seen it too. This will be our secret, and we have to change our meeting place, somewhere else. Somewhere like, the mall.

IN THE BACKGROUND

COURTNEE TURNER HOYLE

This story is dedicated to the law enforcement officers who never give up.

Kaddie balanced the shoebox on her thighs just before it slipped off her cotton slacks again. "How many years have they had the Apple Festival in Erwin?"

Four ladies had been given the responsibility of putting together a photo collage that celebrated the years Erwin had hosted the Apple Festival. It seemed like an easy job, so Kaddie had responded willingly when her husband suggested that she should join the committee. When she arrived, however, she found she was the youngest of the volunteers.

The ladies working with her, Doris, Stella, and Medina, were nice and they accepted her with smiles and bundt cake. They were serious about their work, though, and their knowledge about the festival dated back more years than the thirty that Kaddie had been alive.

The three older ladies, all with gray hair and medical ailments that seemed to give them bragging rights, looked up at her at once. "Forty-five years," Doris said flatly.

Doris was the oldest of the trio, and she had a no-nonsense way about her. She worked at the local library, and her system of balancing cordiality and the monotony of her position was efficient. Stella

18

volunteered a great deal of her time to the local women's shelter. Kaddie believed it was a job that could make a person lose hope in humanity, but Stella's positive attitude shined through when she spoke about her grandchildren or her new designation at the First Baptist Church. Like Kaddie, Medina was a homemaker, and she delighted in telling them about her daughter, Willow, who she must have had a little later in life.

It gave Kaddie hope. So far, she and her husband, Joey, had been unsuccessful in their attempts to conceive, but after several trips to the doctor, her advice had been to rest their minds on the subject.

Kaddie hadn't really put a lot of thought into becoming a mother, and she didn't like the pressure she and her husband received from her younger sister and Joey's mother. Kaddie had just crossed into her thirties, but Joey's mother tapped her wrist like Kaddie's biological clock sat on it every time they told her Kaddie wasn't pregnant yet. Kaddie's younger sister was no better, pointing to her four stair-stepped children and asking when their "older" aunt was going to give them a cousin.

Kaddie took the pressure in stride, but Joey had made appointments for them, first for himself, and then for Kaddie when his doctor revealed nothing was wrong. He had breathed an audible sigh of relief when Kaddie's reproductive system had been deemed normal.

Joey had circled the date on the calendar that her menstruation was supposed to begin for the next three months. "We should be pregnant by then," he'd announced.

She'd disappointed him each month, and the next three circles yielded no results as well.

That was most of the reason Kaddie sat with the Apple Festival Reflection Committee in the library after the doors had been locked for the night. She needed some space from Joey. They'd only been married two years, and the expectation in his eyes every month was too much for her.

The ladies returned to sorting the pictures and laughing at old memories, and Kaddie focused on the photos in her lap, picking up each one and examining it. The images were like time capsules, catapulting her to decades where ladies wore their hair up in tight buns and scolded children who ran around with peace signs on their shirts.

Later pictures showed men with mullets and ripped jeans, while another batch revealed people wearing tons of flannel and boot-cut jeans.

Kaddie had been given the stack with vendors. Medina looked through newspaper clippings, and Stella and Doris shared the responsibility of scanning Apple Dumpling Pageant pictures and other photos of stage performances. Occasionally, they'd lean into one another and whisper. They weren't purposely keeping Kaddie out of their conversations, but she felt awkward as they shared memories about times before Kaddie was born or she was too young to remember.

"Was it in '98 or '99 when it snowed?" Doris asked.

Medina laughed. "I don't remember, but instead of the church sellin' lemonade and ice cream, we were handin' out hot chocolate and apple cider."

Kaddie smiled when she saw a picture of her father selling candy-coated apples in 1977. She was almost certain that was the first year of the Apple Festival.

Her father smiled proudly at whoever was taking the photograph. Next to him, a lady handed a young woman a wood carving etched with a man's face, and people passed, their movements blurred in the image.

The shoebox spilled off her lap and landed on the floor, spilling its contents. The other three women were silent as Kaddie rushed to collect the pictures.

"They weren't sorted, honey, so don't worry about it," Stella said.

Still, Kaddie was embarrassed. She didn't look up as she gathered the items back into the box.

She stopped when her eyes landed on a picture that was similar to the one she'd been looking at when she'd dropped the box. In it, her father was unaware of the photographer, and the lady next to him was handing a woman another one of her wooden crafts. She hadn't noticed it in the first picture, but a man was standing at the side of the booth, watching the women intently. She hurried and located the picture she had studied first. He was in that photo, too.

The man was a little over five feet tall with dark brown hair and green eyes. His black shirt was stretched across a slightly protruding stomach, and his tan slacks bunched at his ankles.

There shouldn't have been anything remarkable about the picture, even though the way he stared at the women receiving the wooden crafts would have frightened anyone, but Kaddie spotted it right away.

The pictures had been taken decades apart. Kaddie knew it, as her father had sold apples during the first years of the Apple Festival, but five years ago, he had purchased a cotton candy machine to use in his booth, too. Even if the picture had been taken five years ago, it still wouldn't make sense.

The man in both pictures was unmistakably the same person, but he looked unaffected by time. There were no wrinkles on his face or other signs of aging.

How could a person look the same for over forty years?

* * *

A tap at the door startled the women, and Doris grabbed her chest. Joey stood outside, and when Kaddie met his eyes, he waved at her.

Kaddie opened the door, hearing the bells jingle over her head. Her husband was dressed in his police uniform, his spiky, blond hair flat in places on his scalp.

"Do you need a ride home?" he asked.

Kaddie had walked from their house three blocks away, but the sun had been touching the mountains when she arrived at the library, and now it was dark and the air was crisp. She nodded her head, even though she wasn't ready to leave.

"Did you find anything interesting?" Doris said as Kaddie grabbed her purse.

"Maybe," she answered honestly. "Could I take some pictures home with me to consider?"

Medina and Stella looked at Doris, and the lady nodded. "Go right ahead."

Kaddie tucked the pictures she had been studying into her purse and left with her husband.

On the way home, she could tell Joey was upset about something. After gently talking to him when they finished dinner, he revealed the source of his stress.

"I responded to a call before I came to get you," he began. "The place was filthy, and three kids under five years old were locked in a bedroom. Their mother was making meth with her boyfriend in the kitchen."

Kaddie's hand went to her mouth. "Those poor children!"

Joey nodded. "They had these far away looks in their eyes. The damage was already so deep."

"But they're out of there, right?"

Joey scrubbed his face with his hands, lifting the front part of his blond hair. "Yeah. They're in foster care. Hopefully, they can all go to the same home."

Kaddie agreed. She couldn't imagine how scared she would have been if she had been in their positions, and she refused to think about what it would have been like to have been separated from her sister.

She ran her hand over his back, rubbing tense muscles and edging him closer to her. "I know you're worried about the children, but you helped them today."

"I hope so," he returned. "I hope I didn't put them in another bad situation."

Kaddie consoled him. "We have good families here. They'll go to a good home."

"Maybe. But they may not all go to the *same* home."

Joey and Kaddie spent the rest of the evening curled up in each other's arms. They watched a show on television and let the noise drown out their thoughts.

Kaddie's mind kept going back to the children. She wondered if they understood their circumstances and hoped they'd receive proper physical, mental, and emotional care.

She forgot about the man in the picture until the next morning.

* * *

Kaddie enjoyed easy mornings with her husband. They were both early risers, and they happily shared the weather and their thoughts around the breakfast table.

Joey left for work, and their laughter faded from the empty house, leaving her with silent furniture and chores to keep her company. She decided to forgo the chores, and she took out the pictures from the previous night.

Kaddie had wanted the man to look different in the light of day, but his eyes still seemed to narrow on the women in both of the pictures. It seemed he almost hated them, and it gave her chills.

Kaddie tried to search for the man using his description. Her criteria were too vague, but she landed on something more interesting.

"Another Erwin Woman Goes Missing During Town's Festival," she read aloud. Her voice cut through the still house.

Another? she thought. Kaddie had heard about missing persons, especially after marrying a police officer, but she didn't remember a case that had rattled her.

Kaddie picked up her purse on her way out the door. There was always one place she went when she had a question about her hometown, and she wasn't going to waste another moment getting there.

* * *

"Kaddie-did!" her father called out when he saw her. He was the only one who issued the endearment, as she had barked at anyone who had tried to call her the nickname. Even though her blonde pigtails were now a short, brown bob, it made her feel as special as the little girl carrying a loose bouquet of wildflowers as she ran into her father's arms.

"What's up?" he asked, after they'd settled at the kitchen table with two cups of black coffee. Kaddie couldn't hide her impatience, but she was careful with her questions. Her dad would tell her what she wanted to know, but he was protective, so she had to phrase her inquiries just right.

"Do you know about missing women from the Apple Festival?"

His mouth pressed into a thin line. "Did Joey tell you about another one?"

Another one? she thought again. She couldn't remember that many missing women in Erwin.

Kaddie didn't watch the news or read about it all the time, but she was certain she would have learned about it from Joey. She decided not to answer.

"I asked him not to tell you."

Her father rubbed his temples. "Do you remember when I kept you and your sister home at night during the weekend of the Apple Festival?"

Kaddie nodded. She'd snuck out and partied at a friend's house during one of those nights, and it was the only time her father had caught her. He must have been keeping a closer eye on her during that time.

"I wasn't trying to be mean to you," he went on. "I was only trying to protect you."

"From what?" Kaddie asked automatically.

"On the first night of the Apple Festival every year, a woman goes missing. They never find them, and they can't link their disappearances. Some of them could've run off and started new lives, but there were two or three who were solid members of the community."

"Why didn't I hear about it?"

"I imagine you did hear about some of them, but it would have seemed random."

Kaddie was a little perturbed by her father's overprotectiveness, but she tried to keep the edge out of her voice as she asked him more questions. "Why were you so worried about me?"

He looked up at her, shocked. "You're a woman."

"But I don't remember seeing anything about missing girls or teenagers."

He looked at his mug. "You know, people are crazy, and who knows why they do what they do? The first year of the festival, the sheriff in the town ran off, and everyone wondered if he was the one takin' the women. Sheriff Doyle was quiet, and a lot of people thought his green eyes made him look like a snake."

Her father's comment about green eyes reminded Kaddie about the pictures in her purse. "Hey, Dad, I found some pictures—" she started, but the doorbell cut her off.

He held up his finger and jogged to the door. Kaddie heard the change in his voice, and she knew who it was before the lady was led into the room.

Kaddie's father had a crush on a tall, brunette woman, but she had never given him a reason to inflate his infatuation with her. The woman was in her late forties or early fifties, and Kaddie's father was in his sixties. She was almost certain the woman dated younger people.

"Ag's here," her father announced with a broad smile.

They exchanged pleasantries, and Kaddie excused herself. Ag was there to consult with her father about his business, and Kaddie felt like she was in the way.

Her father had given her just enough information. And she planned to use it.

* * *

The first day of the Apple Festival was crisp. The festival had been scheduled during the first week of October, and the sun didn't warm the air much above sixty degrees.

Several blocks of downtown Erwin had been sectioned off for the event. Vendors sold their wares on the left and right of the street while patrons walked the length of the road.

It had surprised her father when Kaddie took a seat at his booth, but he welcomed her company and her help. Surprisingly, there was a large demand for candy apples and cotton candy in the early morning hours, and they stayed busy.

Her father liked to ask the people he didn't recognize about their occupations and where they called home. They met lawyers, surgeons, and truck drivers, but most of the early-morning crowd was retired. Her father's patrons hailed from as far as Texas, California, and Canada, and Kaddie was always amused that their small town had the power to attract people from so far away.

Sometime around noon, Kaddie's eyes drifted to the craft vendor beside her. She walked over to the lady who was carving a face on a walking stick.

"Do you have any more like that?" she asked.

"I do!" the lady responded cheerily and pointed to a basket of walking sticks. Kaddie chose one and paid for it. Before she left, she noticed a figure looming around the booth. She pretended not to see him and slipped behind the booths. It was still early, and everyone was using the street to walk down the length of the festival.

"Hey, don't I know you?"

The figure jumped and turned carefully, measuring her with his green eyes. "I doubt it, kid."

It had been a long time since someone had called her a kid, and it threw Kaddie off. She recovered and said, "I'm Kaddie, Limey Wilson's daughter." She pointed to the booth beside them. "He owns the candy apple business."

The man carried a cup and he spit into it. Bits of tobacco dotted his lower lip.

"I know Limey, but I never met his kid."

The man turned away, but Kaddie stopped him. "You never told me your name."

He chuckled without mirth. "I thought you said you knew me."

Kaddie dropped her pretense. "I saw you in a couple of pictures, but you never seem to get older."

The man's thin lips spread into a smile. "Good genes, I guess."

He started to walk away again, and Kaddie yelled after him, "No wrinkles in forty-five years?"

He stopped, but he didn't turn around. Kaddie persisted. "What do you know about the missing women?" she yelled, and several people stared at her from through the booths, clearly irritated by her outburst.

The man fisted his hand, closing it around the styrofoam cup. Tobacco juice dripped down his arm.

"I know you better be careful," he told her.

"Kaddie-did!" her father called, demanding her attention. He'd walked around his booth to look for her. "Can you help me for a minute?"

By the time she looked back, the man was gone.

* * *

Joey got home early, and he and Kaddie made dinner together. It was only a simple spaghetti dish but working in the kitchen with her husband was fun, and she hoped their happy banter would continue through the night.

She was pleasantly surprised when Joey brought out a dice game. "We haven't played that in ages!"

"That's because you always kick my butt when we play," he joked.

Kaddie's phone vibrated in her pocket, and she tried to ignore it. After her father had told her about his attempts to "keep her safe" by telling Joey to keep an eye on her during the first night of the Apple Festival, she hadn't felt like calming his nerves. His fears weren't unfounded, but his methods were sneaky.

She'd been slightly rattled after her conversation with the man from the photographs, but she'd dismissed it. She'd spoken to him, and he'd seemed harmless. Before she'd had time to truly analyze their conversation, Joey had walked through the door and danced her around the room.

Kaddie accepted that Joey was with her because her father had requested it, and it didn't bother her until she realized that Joey was letting her win the game. She thought back to the last time they'd played it, and she was almost convinced that they hadn't played since the first night of the Apple Festival during the previous year.

"You're only spending time with me because my father told you to," she accused.

The good mood left the room like a wind had blown through and carried it away. Joey stared at her, the cup of die in his hand.

Kaddie thought about what her husband should be doing. He was an officer on a force with strained resources. *What had he done in order to stay with her at a time when the town needed him?*

She thought about the late nights he'd worked for the last month, and the sad dinners she'd had alone, often going to bed before he was home. "You worked later so you could stay with me tonight," she said, fully realizing the hardship her father had placed on her husband.

"I want to be with you," Joey countered weakly.

Kaddie's phone vibrated again, reminding her that she had a text message from her father that she hadn't checked, and it was too much for her. She stormed out the door without a backward glance.

Joey called after her, but he couldn't chase her right away. He'd slipped out of his work pants to get more comfortable, and he wouldn't run out in his boxers.

Kaddie walked down familiar streets without a destination in mind. The Apple Festival had closed for the evening, and the booths were covered. It almost seemed like small ghosts lined each side of Main Street. Even though downtown was closed during the night of the festival, Kaddie crossed onto the sidewalk that led down the left of the street. It was a little darker, and she hoped her husband wouldn't see her. She needed to be alone to—

To what? What did Kaddie hope to prove by running out of her house in the middle of the night?

She shook her head. It had been foolish to leave the house, especially before she'd grabbed a coat or her car keys. She wore a sweater, but it hardly helped once her adrenaline wore off. She turned around, beginning an apology in her head that she planned to tell her husband when she arrived home.

She saw Joey running down the sidewalk. She'd almost stepped into the glow of the streetlight when someone grabbed her from behind, securing her in the shadows.

* * *

"Kaddie."

Kaddie didn't want to pull out of her dream. She and Joey were on the beach, and sea gulls were screaming at them as they walked hand-in-hand.

"Kaddie." The voice was whispered, but it was insistent. "You gotta get up, girl."

Kaddie's eyes popped open, but it was still dark. The cry of the gulls in her dream became the scrapping of metal, and the smell of the hot sand was replaced by the stench of oil.

"Kaddie! Can you hear me?"

"Yes," she responded weakly.

"Can you get out?"

Kaddie's body was bunched into unnatural angles, and her knee poked sharply into her cheek. She tried to move her hands, but they had been bound in front of her.

"I can't move!" she yelled back. "Help me!"

Fully awake, her heart raced, and her mind wasn't far behind it. She recognized the voice; it was the man she had seen at the Apple Festival.

Why had he taken her? Was he afraid that she'd uncovered his secret?

Even in her panicked state, Kaddie thought about the fear in his voice when he'd called her name. *If he'd tied her up and placed her in her prison, why was he asking her to free herself?*

"I can't," he answered. "I try every time, but I can't."

His words confirmed her suspicions. The man had put her in a dark place, and he had decided to play a sick game where he pretended to rescue her, instead leaving her to die in her cramped prison.

Voices drifted to her and the sound of metal on metal echoed. Footsteps pounded and her place of confinement vibrated with the sound.

"What the—"

"What is this?"

"She's over there!"

Kaddie recognized the last voice, and she waited while the metal around her was jarred and lifted. Even though she couldn't focus on more than the blackness in front of her, she had an intense wave of vertigo. Light filtered into her vision, and someone grabbed under her arms, lifting her out of her uncomfortable position.

She blinked in the artificial light as Joey kissed her face. Kaddie held her arms out, and one of the other officers cut the rope around her wrists with a pocketknife.

As he sawed at her bonds, Kaddie looked at the metal oil container behind her. She had been stuffed into it and left to die.

But that thought was only slightly more horrifying than what she saw next. She was in a storage building, and the entire place was filled with closed containers.

* * *

Her father touched her wrists where the rope had pulled against them and traced the red mark. He had tears in his eyes when he spoke.

"I almost lost you."

29

Kaddie couldn't argue that she'd been on the brink of death, so she patted his hand. "But you didn't."

"If you hadn't had your phone in your pocket—" Joey started, but he couldn't finish.

It had been a week since Joey had led the police to Kaddie, using the location tracker on her phone. Kaddie had been too upset to fully take in the scene around her, and there was still a lot of evidence for the detectives to uncover.

Kaddie had been found in a storage building on the outskirts of town. It was behind a factory, and she guessed the sounds from the business muffled any possible cries from the victims before they suffocated inside a steel drum.

Forty-six steel drums had been found in the building, and only the one Kaddie had been in was empty when they started their investigation. So far, twelve people had been identified, and their families had been informed of their deaths.

Her father and sister had stayed with Kaddie when Joey had to report to work. Kaddie had enjoyed their closeness, even though she'd spent most of the time in her bedroom.

When she wasn't sleeping, Kaddie reflected on the events that had led up to her abduction. She thought about the man she'd met at the festival and how wrong she'd been about him. She'd always trusted her instincts, but she had learned the hard way that people aren't always as good as they seem.

"I picked up the paperwork," Joey said, slipping beside her and sliding a stack of papers over. "We can fill it out later, if you're up for it."

"Is that the foster parent application?" her father asked.

Kaddie nodded. Joey had spoken about the three children who had been pulled from their home again, and Kaddie had suggested taking them into their home. It was a detailed process, but due to the number of children in need, Kaddie and Joey were scheduled for foster care classes the following week.

Her mind drifted back to her attacker, and Joey noticed her mood deflate. "What's wrong, honey?"

At first, she shook her head, wanting the happy atmosphere around the table to lift her spirits, but after her father urged her to speak, Kaddie told them what was on her mind. "Did you catch him? Nobody told me if you caught the guy who—"

"We got him," Joey confirmed. "It was a transient trucker who was married to a woman in town."

"Donna," her father said, filling in the blanks.

Kaddie startled to attention. "She had the booth of wooden crafts beside you at the Apple Festival."

Her father nodded along. "After their divorce, he never gave up on her. He'd ask her every year to come back to him, but she'd refuse."

"Good for her," Kaddie mumbled.

"Each year, he'd secretly retaliate by tracking down one of his ex-wife's female patrons and killing them," Joey told them. "Once he was caught, he confessed to everything." Joey threw up a hand. "I guess he realized he had no way to deny it when we learned his name was on the storage building's lease."

"He couldn't have put those women there the entire time, though," her father said. "That place has only been open for about two decades."

Joey wasn't as forthcoming with the original location of the killer's collection.

"I'm glad I didn't include the pictures of the sheriff in the Apple Festival display," Kaddie said.

"You had a picture of him?" Joey asked.

Kaddie got up from her chair and found her purse buried under a pile of unopened mail. She dug through it until she found the pictures. "I was going to show them to you that day Ag showed up at your house."

Her father took the photos from her, handing one to Joey. Joey shook his head.

"That's not the guy we have in custody," Joey confirmed.

Kaddie's eyes widened. "But he was the one talking to me before you guys got there. He's the one you arrested at the storage building."

Joey put his hand on her arm. "Honey, we didn't arrest the killer until two days after we pulled you out of there. We used the name on the lease to track him down."

"But I heard him," Kaddie insisted.

"That's Sheriff Doyle," her father interrupted, tapping the picture.

"No one's seen him for over forty years."

"Sheriff Doyle?" Joey asked. "Are you sure?'

"Yeah," her father said. "I remember him well."

"His is one of the bodies from the storage building that we've identified," Joey said. "He had his wallet on him."

"You don't say," her father returned.

Kaddie dropped herself into a chair as the men spoke. Her hands and legs were shaking, and she couldn't find her voice.

She'd seen him, and she'd been convinced he was the killer. She remembered begging him to help her and his insistence that he'd been powerless to help every time. Sheriff Doyle must have gotten close to catching the killer the first time he'd committed a murder, and the killer had dispatched him.

"It's a real shame," her father was saying. "He was a fine police officer."

The two men sat silently around the table, in reverence of the sheriff, while Kaddie stared into space. She wondered what they'd say when they found out Sheriff Doyle had been dead for forty five years, but years after his demise, he was in the pictures they held.

Joey and her father would rationalize that it wasn't the sheriff, and they'd dismiss the man as some out-of-town festival goer, but Kaddie knew the truth. Sheriff Doyle hadn't been able to rest until he'd caught the man responsible for his death and the murders of multiple women.

Her husband and father might stare at the photographs without believing it, but Kaddie knew that they were looking at a ghost.

THE HAUNTED BOOKSHOP

JAN HOWERY

Leslie walked in and sat down at the bar of her favorite, local, downtown hangout. She had a small apartment within walking distance, and since she lived just around the corner, she had become a regular at Misfits Bar.

"You seem a little bit quiet, Miss Leslie," the bartender, Walker, said as he served her the drink she always ordered.

Walker was an old-timer at the bar and had worked there for many years. He retired from the army, was in his early 70s, stood six feet tall, wore large, rimmed glasses, and had long gray hair braided in a ponytail. He looked like a 1960's hippy. Walker claimed his daily drink or two kept him young and young at heart. He always wore jeans, a freshly pressed, button-down, collared white shirt, and a smile on his face.

Leslie looked up from her double vodka and gave Walker a weak smile. "I was laid off today," Leslie said sadly and slowly sipping her drink.

"That's too bad," Walker replied. "The distribution center is laying people off?"

"Yes. Replaced by a robot," Leslie answered.

"Things are changing too fast," Walker said, shook his head, and walked away to greet another customer.

Leslie Bishop, 29 years old, had worked at the distribution center for six years. She worked there full time right out of college. With a degree in Creative Writing, she couldn't find immediate work, so she applied at the distribution center and was hired. The pay was good, and she was only 20 minutes from work.

As Walker greeted other patrons, Leslie turned around and just stared out the window, looking across the street. Across the street was an old bookstore which had been closed for years. There was a dirty, almost completely covered with debris, sign that read Booker's Books. It was an old sign, and the lettering was caved in at the top. Built in the late '40s, the history and age of downtown was exhibited in the struc- ture of the building. It was adorned with an ornate double front door, two large glass windows, and a second floor with large windows as well.

Walker stepped back over to Leslie and said, "That across the street there...it was an exciting business in its day. That bookstore brought visitors from near and far. Another drink?"

"The building looks to be in fair shape," Leslie said. "What hap- pened? Yes. I'll have another drink...light one."

"Old man William Booker started the bookstore in the early '70s. He had just retired from a government job. Everyone knew he enjoyed reading and selling books. He and his wife had no children and they loved having families and kids come into the shop. But...when his wife passed, he struggled to keep it going. He died years ago and it closed. You're too young to remember. Anyone in their twenties or thirties wouldn't remember. And...anyway...things change you know. Too bad, with the downtown revitalization going on, that someone hasn't looked to bring it back to life," Walker said.

* * *

About an hour later, Leslie finished her second drink. "Thanks Walker. Guess I'll head home," Leslie said and left money on the bar.

"Are you sure? It's still early," Walker asked and smiled.

"Yes. I think I'll go home...and read a good book," Leslie answered and winked.

"Do you like to read?" Walker asked.

"Oh yes. I can get lost in a good book because I can just shut out the world when I'm reading. And that's exactly what I want to do this evening," Leslie said.

"Now Leslie, don't ya worry. You'll find something new and better," Walker said encouragingly. "You're a smart young lady!"

Leslie smiled, waved goodbye, and walked out the door. She glanced over to the old bookstore and stopped for a moment. She saw what appeared to be a man standing inside at the window of the shop. She hesitated and thought, *there's someone in that bookstore!*

Leslie picked up her pace. She walked across the crosswalk to the other side of the street and approached the old bookstore. She stopped, slowly stepped toward the store's window, and peeked through the dusty glass. She saw walls lined with shelves that displayed books from the floor to the ceiling. An old typewriter sat on a table in a corner, and an old cash register sat on a long table near the front.

She reached for the ceramic doorknob and turned it. She gasped when the door opened. Leslie stared inside the bookstore in amazement, but did not see anyone. She slowly walked inside and closed the door behind her.

Look at all these books, she thought. *What treasures!* Leslie slowly made her way over to the wall shelves, staring at all the books. *It must've been so exciting*, she thought. *You can feel the joy and almost hear the voices of excitement. What I would give to have my own bookshop!* She reached out to touch a book when she heard a man's voice from the back of the shop, "Can I help you?"

Leslie froze. She slowly turned and looked toward the sound of the voice. "Is there someone here?" Leslie yelled with a trembly voice.

"Yes! I'm back here." It was a man's voice. "Can I help you?"

Leslie crept down a narrow hallway, through a doorway, and found herself in a large room in the back of the shop. The large room was filled with stacked boxes and tables with books stacked atop them. "Hi Missy! Can I help you?" asked the neatly dressed man peering from behind a tower of boxes.

"I...I...I thought the bookstore was closed. I'm sorry. The door was unlocked, and I was curious, and...I..." Leslie stammered and stared at the man.

"Yes. The shop has been closed a number of years now, " the man replied. "But hopefully, it will re-open again...soon," the man said.

"So, it's going to be opening soon?" Leslie asked. "And...who are you?"

The older gentleman smiled and answered, "You can call me Henry, and what's your name?"

"My name is Leslie," she replied. "Do you work here?"

"Yes. I'm here to get the shop up and running again," Henry replied. "Do you like books?"

Leslie smiled, "Yes. I love to read."

"What kind of books do you like to read?" Henry asked.

"Lots of different genres, but I really like a good mystery," Leslie answered, feeling more relaxed.

She watched Henry remove the books from the boxes and stack them on the tables. He would push his large round glasses up on his nose when he bent over. He was dressed like a college professor with a dress shirt, belted pants, and suspenders. He had very thin gray hair, a mustache and small, groomed, gray beard.

"Henry, did you know the Booker family?" Leslie asked.

"Yes. Quite well," Henry answered. "Everyone in this town knew of the Bookers, and it just seems to be a tragedy not to have this bookshop open again. The downtown is coming to life again, and the mayor is showing support to local businesses with grant money to kick start new businesses here. Do you live here?"

"Yes. Around the corner," Leslie said. "It would be great to have the bookshop open...and maybe have a coffee shop too."

"Hold on Missy. One thing at a time. I've got a lot work ahead of me before I think of expanding," Henry said and smiled.

"Could you use some help?" Leslie asked. "I mean...I just got laid off from my job...and...I need to do something, so maybe I could help?"

"Well then, Missy, you came at the right time," Henry said. "Yes, you're the one to help me. My home is on the second floor, so I'll be here anytime."

For the next few weeks, Leslie worked long days at the shop. Henry sent her on errands, had her order supplies, and attend town business meetings. Passersby waved to Leslie while she was working inside the shop. The town officials, through the grant program, cleaned, repaired, and painted the outside of the building.

After a month, the shop was cleaned, stocked, and ready for a grand opening. "Henry, we did it. Look at this! It is so beautiful. The books, the hardwood floors, the wooden shelves, the artistry on the walls... I've had so much fun! You should be so proud to carry this legacy on for the Booker family."

Henry nodded and smiled.

"Henry, let's go across the street to Misfits, and have a drink to celebrate. How about it?" Leslie suggested.

"Yes. The work is done. But...you go ahead," Henry said. "There'll be another time to celebrate."

"Okie dokie," Leslie said with disappointment.

Leslie walked into the Misfits Bar and found her usual seat at the bar.

Walker greeted her, "Haven't seen you for a while. What have you been up to? Do you want your usual?"

Leslie smiled and said proudly, "Yes. My usual. And I've been busy across the street."

Walker looked out the window across the street at the bookshop, and asked, "The bookshop? I've seen all the improvements. Wasn't sure who was doing all that, but it sure does look good. Did you buy it?"

"Buy it? No, I've just been working there," Leslie answered. "I've been helping Henry get the bookshop ready to open."

Walker looked at Leslie as if he had seen a ghost. "Henry?" Walker asked. "Did you say...Henry?"

"Yes. His name is Henry, and he lives upstairs," Leslie replied. "I think that he's a distant relative."

"Henry?" Walker asked again.

"Yes! Henry! Why do you keep asking that?" Leslie asked impatiently.

"Well...Henry was old man Booker's name," Walker said slowly.

Leslie turned pale. "You told me his name was William," Leslie snapped.

"Yes," Walker answered. "His name was William James Henry Booker. Look at the sign over the shop. Now that the town has removed the debris and cleaned it up and painted it, you can read all of the old sign. What do you see?"

Leslie looked at the sign and clearly saw the stone engraved letters on the building. WJH Booker was on the top line and Booker's Books was clearly legible below his name. "I never noticed that before," Leslie said quietly.

"Probably not. It was all covered up. You can see it now," Walker said.

"Well, it must just be a coincidence. Henry and I have worked every day in the shop for weeks, cleaning, inventorying, and getting the shop ready to open. And besides, Henry lives upstairs in the apartment on the second floor."

"Really?" Walker asked surprised. "That's where old man Booker... Henry...and his wife lived."

By now Leslie was getting a little spooked.

"You know Leslie, we stay here in the bar until the wee hours of the morning, and..." Walker hesitated, "I've never seen any lights on over there on the second floor."

Leslie turned and stared out the window at the old bookshop. It looked brand new. It was as if it had taken on a new personality. "But you can see all the work we've done. Walker...maybe you just haven't noticed the lights on," Leslie said.

"Nope. I would've noticed lights on over there," Walker said.

"Well, I didn't do all that work by myself. I had help. He's a man in his sixties or so and has thin gray hair and a mustache with a beard. He's got to be a relative," Leslie said defensively.

"Do you know that he's a relative? Did he say that?" Walker asked.

"Well...no, he didn't say that. I just assumed he was, but he said that he knew of the Booker family," Leslie said slowly.

Suddenly, Leslie broke out into a loud laughter and asked, "You think that I've been working with the ghost of old man Booker all these weeks? Tell me that's not what you think. Guess we'll see when we have the grand opening next week and he shows up!"

Walker smiled, winked, and walked away to greet his new customer.

The next few days, Leslie didn't go to the shop. All the work was done, and it was agreed that she would come by the day before the grand opening. So, on the day before of the grand opening, she got up and arrived at the shop early.

The door was unlocked as usual. She walked in and called out to Henry. "Henry, are you down here?" she asked.

There was no answer. As she walked down the narrow hallway through the doorway to the back room, she called out again, "Henry! Are you here?"

About that time, someone was yelling from the front door. "Is anyone here? I'm looking for a...Miss Bishop. Hello? Is anyone here?"

Leslie turned and walked back to the front of the shop and said, "Hello. I'm Miss Bishop."

Standing in front of her were two men, dressed in business suits. Both appeared to be in their mid-30s. "Miss Bishop, I'm the town Mayor, Mr. Hess, and this is the tax assessor, Mr. Huett. We need to discuss something with you."

"Okay," Leslie said nervously. "What's wrong?"

"Well, there's nothing really wrong," Mr. Hess said. "We need to get your signature on some papers."

"Yes. These are tax papers and the deed to the property," Mr. Huett interjected.

"What do you mean? What property?" Leslie asked.

"This property," Mr. Huett answered.

"There's a mistake," Leslie said. "I'm not the owner. The owner is deceased, and his relative is in the back of the shop. I'll get him."

"No ma'am. William J.H. Booker stopped by the office a few weeks ago, with the tax foreclosure notice in his hand. We tried to find relatives with the aid of our attorney to no avail, and we had to wait the limited time before we could move forward with the sale of the property. So, as the time ended, we gave notice that this property was being sold in a tax lien sale," Mr. Hess explained. "Mr. Booker just showed up and paid for everything in cash. And he applied for an additional grant for the expansion for the bookshop to have a coffee shop. The grant was approved."

"Yes. And Mr. Booker paid the past due taxes and provided a deed that's made out to you," Mr. Huett interjected. "It's all legal. He brought the deed with him and it is signed over to Leslie Bishop. He said that we could find you here today."

Leslie was overcome with shock. "Henry!" Leslie yelled and ran down the hallway to the back of the shop. "Henry! Where are you?"

Leslie looked around the back room full of boxes and books but saw no one. "Henry?" she asked quietly.

Slowly, Henry peered from behind a stack of books, pushed his glasses up on his nose, and said, "Now, it's time to celebrate! And have that coffee shop too!"

With a smile and wink...Henry was gone!

CONNIE THE CAT LADY

LINDA HUDSON HOAGLAND

Connie stepped out onto the patio to survey the quiet, dark hillside behind her home as she did each night before retiring. She looked up to bid goodnight to the moon and the stars, as was her habit, but was suddenly surprised by a startling, high-pitched, cat-like yowl off in the distance—a brief yowl that ended abruptly and then left the night dead silent.

There were no sounds of wildlife or people, which was peculiar for an early fall evening when there were always noises of nightlife.

She felt totally alone, like she was the only person left alive in her world. That wasn't a good feeling for a widow who shared her residence with no one except her cats. Sometimes she felt the only reason she continued to live after her husband's death was because her cats needed someone to feed them.

She had her three indoor cats: Jughead, a handsome black and white male of fifteen years; Cloudy, his sister, who was covered with white and gray clouds; and Wild Child or Fatty (said lovingly) to the feline female with a mostly blue-gray coat trimmed in white, who was the baby of Misty—another littermate to Jughead and Cloudy.

Connie was destined to keep the three cats until they passed on or she did; whichever came first. Of course Connie worried about her

41

indoor kitties, but she knew they were well taken care of. It was her outdoor kitties, the small feral black and white mother cat and her three babies, that worried her most.

Girl was what Connie had called her since the beginning when the cat first appeared on her patio as a kitten. No amount of coaxing could persuade Girl to allow Connie to touch her.

Two years passed and two litters of kitten had entered Girl's world of surviving on Connie's patio and beneath her neighbor's outbuilding.

Girl had with her daily a kitten from her first litter that Connie named Bandit because of the odd markings on his face and two tiny babies called Little Blackie and Spot. As the name signified, Little Blackie was completely black as far as Connie could tell, and Spot was marked with spots of black and white.

Perhaps it was the maker of the distant yowl that was taking all of the stray cats in the area. Or perhaps someone was ridding the world of pesky cats with poison, which was what Connie thought had killed big Blackie who was a domesticated cat without a home.

The lady who used to live next door to Connie was a cat lover, too. She had two indoor cats, but because she was planning to move to another state into an apartment where no more than two cats were allowed, she left Blackie to be cared for by Connie. She had already had him neutered, so he was happy to stay around and soak up all of the attention Connie had to offer.

One morning when Connie was running out of the front door to go to work, she saw that Blackie was still laying on the rocking chair. She didn't have time to investigate his lack of movement. It looked to her as if he didn't get off the rocking chair to eat his breakfast.

Connie worried about him as she started her drive to Lewisburg, West Virginia, for a few days to visit a friend from her high school days. At the end of her two hour drive the worry about Blackie was so domineering in her thoughts that she called her neighbor to see if he would check on the cat.

"I already did that, Connie. I saw that he wasn't moving and his food dish was full. He was dead. I'm so sorry to have to tell you that," said the solemn neighbor. "I took the body away and disposed of it."

"Thanks, John. I was so afraid he was dead," Connie said as she struggled with the tears that were going to roll down her cheeks no matter what she did to stop them. Even though Blackie was an outside stray, she still loved him and would miss him.

Connie's visit with her friend was nice, but Connie was glad to get back home to take care of her feline children. She had paid her neighbor to feed and water the creatures that were inside the house as well as the drop-in visitors outside, but she knew that was not the same. John didn't particularly like cats, but he was glad to give Connie a hand.

Connie suspected that the woman who bought the house next door didn't like the fact that stray cats hung around the place at all times. She was not aware that the previous owner had been a cat lover.

* * *

Connie introduced herself to her new neighbor a few days after she moved into the house that was located to her left, while Connie's friendly, helpful neighbor lived on the right.

"I'm Alice and I'm glad to meet you," the woman told Connie, but the look in her eye betrayed her. She was not happy to be interrupted from whatever she was doing.

"I hope you like living here. We are all older people and we always want to welcome new people into our community. Do you have any questions that I might be able to answer for you?" Connie asked as she tried to be a good neighbor.

"Yes, I do have a question. Where have all of these cats come from?" Alice asked with a grimace.

"I have three cats, but they are all old and stay in the house most of the time. All of the others you see roaming around are strays and some are feral. I feed them to keep them from tearing up everyone's trash," Connie explained.

"What can I do to make them disappear?" Alice asked.

"I don't think you can. I've called the county animal control officer for help, but he said I would have to capture the cats and he would schedule a pick up date. I can't even get close to some of the feral cats. I wouldn't want to see them euthanized; so, I feed them.

That gets expensive for me because I'm on a limited income that is Social Security and a small pension, but I've managed to do it. You can help feed them if you like," Connie said with hope in her heart.

"Never going to happen. I just want them gone," answered Alice with a snarl.

"Are you allergic to cats? I see that you are wearing a medical alert," asked Connie.

"Not cats, I just don't like cats. I'm allergic to shell fish," replied Alice.

"It must be a bad allergy," said a pensive Connie.

"It is," said Alice.

* * *

Connie felt that the death of Blackie could be traced back to Alice. She also thought that the disappearance of about six other strays could be traced to Alice. Of course, it did cut down a bit on the cat food bill, but that was not the way Connie wanted to do it.

How am I going to stop her from killing the cats?

Connie and Alice did not become friends. They did not even acknowledge each other when they were within shouting distance. With the death of Blackie possibly by poisoning, Connie thought Alice should be made to pay in some way.

It was getting near Christmas and Connie was in a baking mood. She rustled up all of the ingredients she need to make her good oatmeal raisin cookies that most of her friends seemed to like. She made several batches to give away as gifts with the addition of a finely ground, secret ingredient that she sifted into the special batch for a special friend.

Each batch was decorated with a fancy bow attached to the tin full of cookies. Her special friend was the only one to receive a tin with both the bow and an artificial poinsettia.

Alice wasn't home when Connie went to deliver her gift, so she placed the tin of cookies at her side door where she always entered. She signed the card with "Happy Holidays from your Neighbor."

Just before the New Year, Connie saw an ambulance pull into Alice's driveway. Before too long it left without red lights or sirens.

The article in the newspaper said Alice was discovered by a visiting friend. The cause of death was an allergic reaction identified by the medical examiner as shell fish. It was designated as an accidental death.

Connie smiled.

THOSE WHO CAME BEFORE

LORI C. BYINGTON

A soft whisper of undecipherable words wafted by Leta Rhea's left ear. She thought a late mosquito had buzzed too close, so she waved her left hand randomly to shoo the creature away. The odd whisper then shooshed by her right ear and faded away as quickly as it came. Leta looked to her right for the annoying insect and swished her right hand in front of her face. She saw no bug at all, let out a "huhhh," and continued her nightly walk around her neighborhood.

The early October air was crisp, but the first frost had not glistened on the roofs or yards, as of yet. A few feet into her walk along Mosby Lane, Leta saw a woolly worm valiantly trying to cross to get into the grass. She gently picked up the fuzziness and carried it to where it wanted to go. She noticed the colors of the woolly worm, smiled to herself, and thought, *well, the Race of the Woolly Worms in nearby Qualla Valle, North Carolina sure did not disappoint. The critters' fronts were brown, the middles were black, and the backs were brown again.*

The wives' tales, almanacs, and Native American legends handed down, rarely missed predicting the weather at any time of year, so a lack of early frost was not uncommon to East Tennessee. According to such long-trusted sages, "Watch the colors of the woolly worms and count the dew frosts in August to see how bad the winter will be." The tell-tale signs include, "A brown front on the woolly worm means warmer weather at the start of the winter; the black in the middle means cold weather in the middle of the winter; and the brown at the end means a warm end to winter."

Leta glanced at the sky, noticed the early, harvest full moon, which looked a bit off, and checked her watch. The time was 7:30 PM, and she still had to get steak and gravy on the stove, so she walked with a purpose to get home. The neighborhood was great for exercise because many of the streets were up a hill and down a hill. She turned right off Mosby Lane onto Carmack Road. She kept a good pace but noticed the air all of a sudden felt heavy, as if a wieldy, wet, wool blanket had been tossed on top of her head. The sun was waning low before Leta could end her trek, so the sky was still in an orange and crimson glow. No extra light, save the lights of neighbors' homes, shown on the street. All at once, she shuddered. She glanced up at the clouds covering the moon, but it looked like God had randomly thrown a bucket of scarlet paint over the night sky. She didn't think a thing about the moon and started walking again. As she rounded the corner of Carmack to walk up the hilly yard to her house, she heard a familiar, "Arrrroooo, yip, yip, yip, arrrroooo!"

She stopped to listen, unafraid, because she knew the coyotes, really coyote and red wolf hybrids, ran their habitual path on the ridge of the Holston Mountains around 7:30 PM every night. Like clockwork, the yipping and howling sounded like a solemn, lost siren-song for eight to ten minutes. Once the hounds found their prey or settled down for the night, the barking stopped—but not at once. Ever so slowly the howling, whimpering, and yipping died off as if an orchestra conductor were waving them from a crescendo to sudden silence. One coy-wolf, the head of the pack, always ended the song by himself as he voiced the last "yip-yip" and drawn out "arrroooo."

Leta and her husband, Ed, agreed they could set their watch by the coy-wolves on their nightly jaunt. Ed always said the "jaunt" was really their hunt, but the canines rarely came closer than their haunting, orchestral wails carried over the wind.

As Leta turned to walk up neighbor Nolan's driveway toward the apple trees in her own back yard, her heart froze and she stopped mid-step. She stared smack-dab into the scarlet eyes of a very large dog. The hairs on her neck prickled and chill bumps ran down her arms as if she had been thrust into a cooler full of the spoils of the fall deer hunt. The beast was clearly much taller than the random coy-wolf that ran the ridge and often across the roads in front of their house. He looked straight at Leta as if to purposely lock eyes. In disbelief and fear, Leta's own blue eyes opened so wide she thought her eyebrows would touch her forehead. The wolf's eyes, the beast *had* to be a wolf, mimicked Leta's, but his eyes were oddly ruby colored and did not flinch in the least at the confrontation. His coat was wet and splotched gray with red-copper, and his tail was a billowy mass of long fur trailing out behind him. His mouth was ajar but no hint of exhalation emerged. There was no vapor of hot air or any signs of an animal as large as this taking a breath. Leta's eyes widened more as she tried to process what she thought she saw.

Suddenly, Leta heard a lone "whoooooo" coming from the direction of the old pond that once quenched the thirst of thousands of wildlife, natives, and, later, Civil War soldiers on their trek to defend their homes. As she turned to look toward the faint howling, a strong rush of wind flew past her and almost knocked her down. Leta got a whiff of wet dog fur and mud, but when she turned back to look where the beast had been—he had vanished. She shuddered again, as if from the cold, but this time beads of sweat formed on her forehead and began to run down her face. She shook her head to clear her disbelief, and walked up the yard to the driveway.

"I did not just see a giant red wolf under our apple trees, with ruby eyes, glaring at me! I need to get supper on the stove and calm down," Leta said out loud and shook her head once again.

When Leta got inside the house and to the den, she looked out over the back deck to see if she could see any sign of the wolf. The blood moon was bright, and no clouds eclipsed its face. The pine trees swayed as the wind blew, and the chimes on the deck jingled a happy turn in time.

"I must be losing my eyesight and my mind," Leta said to herself as her husband, Ed, stomped in from the garage into the den.

"What are you talking about?" asked Ed. He had a quizzical look on his face and obviously raised his gray-black eyebrows on purpose as he asked the question.

"Well, you will not believe me, but I saw a huge red wolf under the apple trees. He was a lot bigger than the Holston Mountain coy-wolves we see running around. He had enormous, ruby colored eyes, and when he should have been breathing, because his mouth was open, nothing came out. There was no mist or steam or anything to show breath," she answered, scratched her head, and wrinkled her forehead.

Leta raised her eyebrows in recollection, "When I was about to finish my walk, I heard a lot of howling, moaning, and yipping, louder than normal, but I assumed our coy-wolves were running the ridge to hunt and bed down. The moon was redder than the usual harvest moon also. Did you see?"

Ed shook his head to answer "no," pursed his lips, put his hands on his hips, and looked out the sliding glass door to the back yard and toward the neighborhood pond. The moon was clearly a lot redder than the traditional harvest moon, and a weird fog had formed where the neighbors' yards met the old pond. Ed blinked a few times to make sure he saw real fog, which is normal in East Tennessee in the fall. When the air is colder than the water, steam forms and hovers, ghost-like, over any pond, lake, stream, or creek.

"I don't know what you saw, but the pond sure looks crazy with the blood moon reflected, and an eerie cloud is hovering over. I have never seen that before," Ed remarked. "The fog looks like it is growing! Come see!"

Leta walked quickly to where Ed was standing in their den and looked where he pointed. She froze in disbelief.

"There's the red wolf! See how big he is! Wait, is he forming from the fog?!" Leta squeaked as she squinted her eyes.

Ed looked at Leta, shook his head, a clear smirk on his face, and looked back toward the pond. His eyes grew as big as half-dollars and *he* blinked hard, twice.

"Lord love a duck and holy what in Pete's name is that?" Ed almost yelled.

Leta and Ed studied the pond, then glanced at each other in agreement, and opened the sliding glass door to tip-toe out for a closer look.

They were shocked by the sight. The fog not only grew and seemed to form the body of the wolf, but the miasma was moving in waves and undulating back and forth across the whole pond. The breeze had picked up and the sun had set, so the only light was the odd harvest moon, which was bright enough to light up the whole of the pond. Suddenly, howling, yipping, and barking, from what sounded like a hundred wolves, filled the air and the sound danced with the fog. This caterwauling was not normal and not the familiar coy-wolf nightly routine. The intonation flowed back and forth, rose and fell in rhythm and was almost deafening. The air had grown muggy, as if rain had pelted the surroundings, but no rain had fallen. The fog had a life of its own but still kept the shape of a massive wolf. The specter turned its head straight toward Leta and Ed as if he were focused on them. The eyes of the creature were sparkling crimson and pierced through the mist. The beast's mouth was ajar and silver fangs were visible.

Leta and Ed could not take their eyes off the creature. The phantom wolf held them in a trance just as Dracula did with Lucy in Stoker's novel. The beast did not blink at all and kept his gaze focused on the Rheas.

Ed gawked at the vision he was seeing, breathed in, let it out, and said, "Remember when I told you Granddad was part Cherokee? Granddad's mother was half Cherokee, and he told Pap stories of tribal beliefs and rituals. I remember Granddad saying the month of October was a special time, but I don't remember the whole story. I wonder..."

Before Ed could finish, the mist and the giant wolf began roiling and whirling as a small tornado landed in the middle of the pond. The trees swayed so far, they looked as if they would upend by the roots. Ed, wide eyed, looked at Leta, but she only nodded and stared at the scene before them. She was clearly entranced. Ed swung his head to look at the pond just in time to see a white cloud descend to the bank. The wolf-beast looked away, broke the trance-like stare, and changed form in front of the Rheas' eyes. The animal became flesh and bones. He was no longer a mist. His fur was full and reddish, as Leta saw earlier, and his tail billowed out behind. The wolf, clearly whole and still monstrous, glistened in the moonlight. He flashed his bright ruby eyes once and stared back directly at Leta and Ed.

"Ohhhh, in heaven's name...?' Leta began.

"Ummm, I think we are dreaming," Ed said, with hesitation. "But we are not asleep, and we clearly are not dead," he shrugged and whispered to Leta.

The fog began to swirl again with force, the October moon began to spin counter clockwise as its color changed from the scarlet to yellow-orange, and the mist vanished from the surface of the pond. Abruptly, the wolf looked to his right, backed up a few feet from the edge of the pond where he stood, stretched his right leg out in front and bent his left leg under his belly. He tucked his head under his chest in a bow and let out a loud "whoooo-whoooo-yip-yip-arrroooo." The gusts forcefully carried the call over the pine and oak trees surrounding the pond. The coy-wolves, well-hidden in the nearby mountains, immediately responded in earnest.

Ed and Leta, eyes wide, looked at each other.

"What in the tarnation is going on?" Ed whispered.

Leta looked from her husband back toward the pond and blinked several times.

"I don't know, but I want a closer look," she answered in a louder voice.

"Leta! Are you crazy?" Ed asked. "Wait!"

Leta made her way to the right side of the deck to get a full-on view of the pond. Ed followed, hesitantly. They unconsciously breathed in unison and tried to be quiet. Blasts blew from the east stronger than before, and the light from the weird moon shown brighter out over the pond. The giant wolf swished his tail back and forth quickly but stood motionless in his bow. Leta and Ed could not take their eyes off the scene. Neither one spoke and both tried not to blink. Magically, the swirling fog parted a few feet in front of the spot where the wolf reverently bowed. A perfect oval slowly formed at the water's edge, grew to at least six feet in height, and a golden light burst from the opening directly in front of the bowed beast.

Ed swallowed hard, barely breathed, and repeated, "What the...is going on?"

Leta, mesmerized, shook her head as if to clear cobwebs and turned toward Ed. "I don't know, but I have goose bumps all over, and I know we are not dreaming," she whispered.

The Rheas were mesmerized at the sight before them.

"Ed! Look at the hole in the air! The light is spinning inside and I see a figure!" Leta said aloud and shook Ed's left sleeve of his green flannel shirt.

Ed looked to where Leta had nodded. The light in the oval became as bright as the fabled Sirius star. The giant canine raised his head from his bow, barked "woof, woof, woof" three times, made a low, guttural growl and sent an ear piercing "arrrroooo-yip-yip" across the pond. The unearthly sound caused the limbs of the oaks to sway wildly, which sent amber and brown leaves down in droves. The surface of the pond rippled with waves to rival the white caps of the Atlantic Ocean.

Leta and Ed glanced at each other, then back to the pond and squinted to better see. "Sshhhhh," Leta whispered. "Something is happening!"

Slowly, from the orange and yellow oval an apparition of a tall, tan figure stepped. He wore a warrior's head band with two bald eagle and two red-tailed hawk feathers sprouting from all four sides. He had no other clothing save a tan deer pelt cinched at his waist by thin, black bear hide straps. On his arms above the elbows were bands of sleek, dark leather. In his right hand he carried a long spear clearly whittled from white oak. At the top of the spear, a long, gray, sharp arrow head, expertly made from Tennessee shale, was held in place by tightly wound grape vines. Four ebony crow feathers poked down from the vines and swayed in time to the gusts rounding the pond.

"That man looks like to be Cherokee, but how? Where did he come from?" whispered Ed.

Leta shook her head and tried to mentally grasp what they were witnessing, or thought they were witnessing. Were they dreaming?

"Look at his clothes, and is that a spear with feathers?" she asked and shook her head as if that joggle would help.

As Leta spoke, the Cherokee faced the giant wolf and bowed low in return. The man pounded the end of his spear into the ground four times and then rose to his full height. Ed and Leta saw the dust float up from the ground and dissipate into the mist. The man raised his right hand, said something to his animal brother in an old language Ed and

Leta did not understand, and turned directly toward them. The wolf then turned to face the shocked couple who stood frozen in their spots.

"Ed...what are they doing?" Leta almost shrieked. She quivered from both fear and excitement, so much that her teeth rattled together.

Ed shook his head but did not take his eyes off the ethereal sight before him. Before he could answer both Cherokee and giant beast nodded their heads as if to acknowledge the Rheas. The wind died down, the pond's water swirled slower and the pine and oak trees held their ground. Leta noticed the beast's eyes were no longer scarlet but a piercing sky-blue. The man's smooth face shown softly in the light from the harvest moon, which had mysteriously changed from blood colored to the normal orange of October.

Leta blinked, rubbed her eyes, and stared again at the pair of beings who stood not ten yards from the deck of the house.

"Ed..." Leta began, but before she could finish her statement, Ed shook his head and raised his right hand in an ancient, long forgotten, salute the pair.

The Cherokee and the giant red wolf nodded, once again, then turned toward the pond. Both figures stood still as statues, and the pond began to glisten as gold sparkles of light rose from the surface. The wind picked up again, but slowly, not as fierce as before. A tower of white steam rose from the pond. The steam reached the height of the six-foot tall chief, and, together with his animal brother, walked through the golden mist that hovered over the pond. The two, once abundant sentries in East Tennessee, slowly faded into the light.

"Pop, pip, crash, pop!" burst out around Leta and Ed, not only near the pond, but in the Rhea's house as well. As the spirits ended their traditional journey, all light bulbs in the deck lanterns shattered in unison. Leta and Ed ducked automatically to avoid the glass shards.

Leta shuddered from the sudden chill, glanced up from her crouch, wide-eyed, and remarked, "We just witnessed, I think, a ritual we were not supposed to see."

Ed kept his eyes on the pond and quietly nodded in agreement. Without looking at Leta, he said, "I know. Somehow, I know from memories from my ancestors."

Not a minute later, nearby coy-wolves began a mournful, loud "awoooo-oooo!" The sound was a musical force of life that wrapped around the pond and whooshed loudly over the Rhea's home as if a tornado had barely missed the chimney. Ed and Leta *felt* the cries, and howls *physically* whizz over them as they hugged, cowered low on the back deck of their house. The ghostly calls clearly carried east toward the nearby Holston Lake and dove straight into the surrounding mountains.

After the rush of haunting sounds and the wolves' singing dissipated, Leta and Ed, still crouched, held to each other to slowly stand. They glanced down at the deck to check the damage from the shattered bulbs, and, in unison, looked toward the crisp, clear October sky. The new harvest moon was a brilliant orange and a bright, gold halo surrounded the surface.

"Ummm, I guess we need to sweep the glass up off the deck," Ed said, methodically.

When Leta began to respond, a lone, haunting "Aroooo! Whoooo! Aroooo-ooooh!" reverberated back from the Holstons where the Cherokee chief and the red wolf returned.

Leta shuddered involuntarily, just as she had when she first saw the red wolf-haint. She let out pent up air as she stated, matter-of-factly, "I am never taking my daily walk again in October unless the moon is normal."

Ed looked toward the calm pond where he and Leta had witnessed a ritual, not allowed to be seen by many. He wrapped his arms around her and stood still.

Ed inhaled deeply through his nose and said softly, "If you do, let me know. I might want to see one of my ancestors with his red-wolf brother again."

THINGS THAT HAPPEN IN THE MOUNTAINS, STAY IN THE MOUNTAINS

PAULINE PETSEL

The smell of hot dogs roasted over a bonfire permeated the air. Their skins split open and a sharp sizzling sound could be heard as their juices met with the fire below. Hot dog buns on the paper plate soon were filled with catsup, mustard, and for some, onions or pickles. Reaching into the large bag being passed around from person to person, potato chips were added to the now overfilled plates.

The flames of the fire sent dancing shadows throughout the campsite, and they seemed to cast weird, sometimes scary or monster looking shadows from neighboring trees and bushes onto the tent walls. This provided a perfect atmosphere for what everyone knew was yet to come. Raccoons who couldn't neglect the smell and activities crept silently toward the group. Some merely found a thing of interest on their own and were caught trying to open bottles or jars sitting off to one side. One or two got brave and crept forward to the awareness of a few individuals who spotted them, and reached out with a gifted morsel in their hand. What is a bonfire without marshmallows to roast? Soon white, fluffy marshmallows started turning a light brown tint but there were always those who caught them on fire and watched the torch they became turn to a charcoal shriveled color. That charcoal had a special taste of its own, and the soggy white then left, was once again caught on fire until every morsel was gone.

Then the time had come—the time everyone waited for. A scary story was to be told around the campfire. Everyone wanted it, but at times there were some who all of a sudden changed their mind.

The setting was perfect. A woodland filled with trees thick enough to hide monsters. The Appalachian mountains towering far overhead with a striking, dark sky, thin wispy cloud here and there, a full moon, and very few stars. To add to the atmosphere, a rabbit scampered through or a wolf howled in the background, sounds that seemed to happen at the most opportune time. In fact, sometimes the storyteller themselves got a shiver or two in their own spine.

And so, the story began...

* * *

First of all, I must tell you, this is more than a story, but rather an account of actual events encountered, of people who were quite similar in interests of hiking and camping as our group around the fire now.

It seems there was a family along with friends who had gone for a walk in the woods. The day was warm with a gently breeze sifting through their hair and ruffling their shirts and pants. The adults walked the trails for exercise and were interested in the beautiful scenery. The children, ranging from six to thirteen, chased one another and looked for wildflowers to pick and make a bouquet to give to their mothers. They chased butterflies and even found a snake much to the pleasure of the thirteen-year-old but not the others, as he chased them with it.

They came to an area where the trail was heading in a downward position, leaving the sky up higher and more trees and shrubs were becoming the norm. Off in the distance was some kind of movement, which at first they thought to be an airplane, but as it came closer all the adults gasped. It couldn't be! That darn thing was a flying saucer! There was no mistaking it. It looked exactly like what pictures in magazines showed and was quite detailed as it got closer and closer. Cameras came out of pockets and bags or from around necks as the group captured what they saw. The children stopped and looked up in amazement. Then all of a sudden, the object made a sharp right hand turn and sped off like greased lightning and was completely gone from sight, leaving the awe stricken viewers with only baffled conversation at the most. They had heard folklore about UFO sightings being attributed to these mountains, but they had no idea they would actually see one, and it sure was no folklore.

Binoculars replaced the cameras as they started scouring the countryside in case they might see more. What they did find was an opening to a cave half hidden behind a mass of bushes but close to the trail. Although it wasn't the adults' idea, it didn't take much coaxing by the children to go inside and explore it. The usual flying bat sweeping down overhead, a mouse scampering for cover, and insects or lizards accompanied their inspection of the area. The unexpected find of both animal and human bones put the group in a different frame of mind. What happened to these people? Why and how did they die? An owl hooted in the far-off distance.

* * *

At this moment, the group listening to the campfire story were transported into the cave from the story, because at the perfect time an owl hooted in the woods behind them.

* * *

After finding the human bones the children didn't run ahead as fast as before, but stuck closer to the adults. A rhythmic sound like beating drums could be heard far off in the distance at which point the kids were actually behind the adults, who were approaching the sound a bit more slowly, but too nosey to forget it altogether. Ahead a sort of glow from a campfire seemed to be flickering and bounding off the dark cave walls and the beating noise of the drums grew louder. They reached a huge boulder which had a convenient hole for the adventurers to peer through at the unfolding scene below. Native Americans sitting cross legged and wrapped in blankets watched as others danced to the beat of the drum players' drums. This was amazing. Here was another tale about the Appalachian Mountains being brought to life right before their very eyes.

But then, something happened that caused the hidden viewers to gasp and look at one another to see if the others saw it too. They quickly put their hands over their mouths so not to be heard and detected by those below. The dancers and drum players disappeared. I mean, *disappeared!* They didn't leave and go somewhere. They just, disappeared as if ghosts and were no longer there as if they had never been. Quickly looking at the Native Americans sitting on the blankets, they discovered that they were tied up and not an audience after all.

In came a whole new set of characters. I can't say 'people', because they were strange looking characters. They didn't look like they were of this world. Their ears were pointed, and they had large heads with gross looking faces and odd shaped noses. This was more than the adventurers could take. With a finger to their lips to indicate being quiet and a pointing movement with the other hand to show the others that they should get the heck back where they came from, the group made an exit as fast as they could. Once outside they made a unanimous vote to leave this area and head back up the trail to higher ground, where only beautiful scenery existed and the sunny light of day. Well, part of that was possible, but they had been on the trail so long that when they reached higher ground, they discovered they went way past the time when they should have returned to where they had started.

The sun was going down and soon would be setting, but after what they just experienced even a darker day in the open was better than being inside a weird, mysterious, scary cave. The day turned out to be more than what they had planned and was sure to be one they would never forget. A couple of the guys had binoculars with night vision, so they searched the area to see if they could find a trail that might get them back to where they parked faster.

One of the men spotted something with his binoculars off the path quite a ways away, but thought it might be a good idea to try to go that direction. It might be a little harder path, but at this point everyone was ready for faster than easy. Still, it ended up being a little more of an issue than they thought. They were soon climbing huge, jagged rocks, and slipping down loose earth out of control. The adults were having enough problems, but the small children were getting cuts and bruises and skinned hands and knees. The logical thing would be to return the way they came and have to put up with being longer than with this being so treacherous, but the landscape made that now impossible. The sky outside was becoming dark and threatening the possibility of incoming rain. What's worse, there now seemed to be a wind starting to blow.

But then finally they had some luck! Just in the nick of time they spotted a cave opening to get some shelter. Though they doubted the luck of *another* cave, it was either that or be pelted and drenched with the now falling rain. They promised they would not be going back into this cave and would leave the minute it was light enough to do so. The men in the group started taking off their shirts to tear and make dressings for some of the cuts that were bleeding. Once again, a couple bats flew over their heads so close that they brushed some of their hair, causing screams as the other cave's influence was taking a toll. A hoot of an owl added to the deteriorating atmosphere, and then on top of it all, creepy crawling bugs seemed to be trying to find shelter too.

They soon wished that was all they had to confront. White moving circles of lights started floating mysteriously in the air. A few at first, then some a little larger. They were very quiet and just seemed to float. From the back of the cave a howling sound echoed and seemed to bounce off the walls. Not again! No way were they going anywhere except to stay right where they were just inside the cave opening! The adults tried to put on a brave front, but they were now experiencing things they had heard rumors of in these mountains, things they never really thought were real. The previous cave was fresh in their minds too, and they wanted out of here just as much as the kids.

They knew what those white things were—they were spirit orbs. But no one knew what those sounds from back further in the cave were, and they weren't about to find out! Whose idea was this? They were in way over their heads and no way to get away from it. A huge roar like a machine, but perhaps only a mud landslide close by, rocked any remaining calm atmosphere there might have been. Then looking out of the cave opening, they saw figures in uniform approaching. They hoped maybe some rangers saw their car in the parking lot and set out searching for them. Maybe that loud sound was a rescue machine of some sort. They watched the figures approaching, wondering how in the world, of all the places on the trail, they could even know where they might find them. But that question was answered fast enough.

Suddenly, the figures disintegrated into thin air! Not one, which might have been explained as being unseen because of the rain, but *all* of the figures just disappeared! *Not again!* It was just like those Native Americans that disintegrated into thin air. Here were more apparitions or ghosts! The kids screamed and cried, and the adults hugged everyone closer. They acted like they were protecting and comforting the children, but in reality they were trying to find comfort of their own.

What ever happened to those people? Did morning come and they found their way safely back to their cars? Or are they still lost at a place of no return and have become a part of the Appalachian folklore held tightly by the mountains?

It is said that those spirit orbs camouflage themselves and can be seen at night by people as merely blinking fireflies or lightning bugs, *but...*which ones are the bugs, and which are spirit orbs?

Will any human bones found by future hikers be people from long ago? Or will bone discoveries be the end of this story revealed? Will future people on the hiking trail that see and greet each other be actual people, or will they too disappear and disintegrate into thin air as they live their new life as apparitions or ghosts of a spirit realm?

So, did they get out the next day and get safely back home? Or are they now a part of the folklore? Only the Appalachian Mountains know for sure! *You* have to decide for yourself, but if you hear a group of people's voices that seem to come to you within the wind, or see children and adults seeming to be there but you can see through them, or you see strange looking fireflies or lightning bugs in the night, *be aware!* You just may be witnessing a ghostly phenomenon.

* * *

The story ended with the campfire scene having changed. The previously tall, orange, flapping, shadow casting flames had died down leaving only a fiery hot clump of bright, orange glowing embers which popped and spit out a spark at times. The camp was darkened except for its glow. The children had gotten into sleeping bags which had been near their side at the start, and were now deep inside with only their heads showing...as if those sleeping bags were some kind of protective shield. An owl hooted again somewhere out in the woods and a bat flew across the scene. A raccoon sat off to one side peering into the group. A soft breeze started to blow and rock the trees gently, causing a soft, strange kind of rubbing sound of the limbs, almost giving the woods some kind of voice of their own. Looking upwards through the clearing of the trees above, the bright full moon cast its moonbeams downward.

Suddenly, what was *that*? Was that a beautiful silhouette of an eagle smack in the center of the moon? It looked sort of different though. Then, a flying saucer shape seemed to take its place.

That ended the camping activity for the night. It was time to bed down and reflect on their wonderful day of activities. Many thoughts filled the minds of those campers as their eyes shifted back and forth in the still of the night, watching every blink of lightning bugs, which now seemed to be everywhere. There were small ones, tiny ones, large ones, and *really* big ones.

It was the end of both the story and of another fun camping trip in the Appalachian Forest...or was it the end?

THE FUNHOUSE

JEFF GEIGER JR.

The carnival only came to the little town of Big Clifty, Kentucky once a year, and it was always the weekend before Halloween. It had all the typical carnival and fair rides: a carousel, bumper cars, a Ferris wheel, and of course the teacups that'll spin you until you inevitably throw up your lunch. And they had the big-kid rides too; the ones that would sling you around nearly eighty feet in the air with only a strap securing you to the seat you're in. You'd think one of those would be the scariest ride there, right? During the day, you would be correct. At night, though, that simply wasn't so.

In Louisville that afternoon, Richie Ward was rushing through the restaurant to get his tables cleared. He was a server and already forty-five minutes late to pick up his girlfriend, Madison Hitchens. He could feel his phone vibrating in his pocket every five to ten minutes, knowing it was Madison wondering where the hell he was and why he wasn't texting her back.

Finally, after his last table had left, he hurried outside and called Madison.

She answered on the first ring. "What gives, Richie? No response for the last—what—hour or so?"

He knew she'd be upset, but he was going to make it up to her. He was going to win her a stuffed animal, get her whatever fried food she wanted, and give her the night of her life at the carnival. It would be a night she'd never forget.

"I'm sorry, Madison. It's been a crazy day here. Two people called in sick and—"

"Can you spare me the explanations and just come and get me?"

"Yes, your majesty. I'm leaving now."

"What'd you say?"

"I said yes, you're mad, I see."

"Not mad. I'm irritated because you're late and haven't been answering my texts."

"That's because—" Richie stopped himself. He knew if he continued it would only exacerbate the situation. "I'm on my way."

Madison was one of the prettiest girls in Louisville. The contours of her face were perfect. With her smooth skin and dark-brown hair, winning pageants was easy, and being the high-school prom queen was even easier. She met Richie a year or so after they graduated high school. She was in line behind him at a bookstore, noticing he was holding the same novel in his hand as she was holding. She waited for Richie to make the move, which he did, of course, right there in line. Richie wasn't like the guys she had dated in high school, though. He wasn't a very big guy, didn't have a lot of money or an expensive car, but they had shared interests, and he could often make her laugh until her eyes watered.

Richie stopped at his house first to change out of his work clothes. He was walking out of the door when his phone vibrated in his pocket again. He pulled it out, reading the text on the screen.

It was Madison. Almost here?

Richie texted back. Be there in a few minutes.

Madison was sitting on a porch swing under the eave when Richie stopped in front of her house. When he saw her walking briskly to his car, he got out in a hurry so he could open the passenger-side door for her.

"What a gentleman," she said, the hint of a smile on her face. "Other than being late."

"Good things come to those that wait, right?" He gave her a smile, hoping it would be a charming one.

She rolled her eyes and sat in the passenger seat. She didn't say anything, just tilted her head toward the steering wheel. Richie closed her door softly and got back behind the wheel.

He took Interstate 65 down to the Western Kentucky Parkway. Richie had put Madison in a better mood with a joke or two. The traffic wasn't too bad, either; they were making pretty good time. Then, after being on the Western Kentucky Parkway for a couple of minutes, they saw traffic stopped up ahead. Richie glanced over to see that Madison's smile had disappeared.

They moved at approximately a turtle's pace for half an hour before finally passing the crash that had caused the traffic jam. With that behind them, they cruised on until they found the exit for Big Clifty.

"I can't believe they decided to have the carnival in such a small town this year," Madison said.

"Probably easier to get whatever permit they need to set up everything," Richie said.

They turned onto Cemetery Road and saw the carnival entrance maybe two hundred yards away.

"Heck of a name for a road," Richie said. "I wonder why—oh, now I see."

To their left was a graveyard with perhaps a dozen tombstones. There wasn't even a fence around them. It was the smallest graveyard Richie and Madison had ever seen.

They found parking in the back of the lot. They'd come late so all the good spots had already been taken. By the time they got their tickets and walked in, it was quarter to five.

"What do you want to ride first?" Richie asked as his eyes wandered around, checking out all the amusement rides.

"Let's start with the Ferris wheel," Madison said, taking his hand. "We'll be able to scope out everything this place has to offer."

Richie nodded, trying not to appear nervous. He didn't exactly have acrophobia, but being high up and looking down always made his stomach churn. He wasn't going to have Madison go on the ride alone, though.

As the Ferris wheel rotated around, Richie saw an empty cart come up.

"Next," the carny said as he opened the door to the cart.

"Finally," Madison said. "Come on, Richie, this'll be fun."

They sat next to each other on one side of the cart. Richie could feel beads of sweat on his forehead. When the Ferris wheel started to rotate again, Richie said, "Shouldn't I sit over on the other side? You know, so we don't tip this thing over?"

Madison almost snorted with laughter. "That's a good one." She wrapped an arm around his, holding him tight. "I'm glad we're finally here enjoying ourselves."

He did enjoy her warmth as she held him close, but as the cart leaned to one side, he only felt the fear of falling to his death. The fear was, of course, irrational. A multitude of people ride Ferris wheels all over the world without falling out. Yet in Richie's mind, it was still a possibility.

They were stopped at the top now. The carny was letting another couple on the ride two hundred feet below them. Richie continued with the fear-is-just-a-joke thing; it was easier for him than trying to hide it.

"Well, we're still alive," he said with a little shake to his voice.

She laughed again, squeezing him tight as she did. Then she leaned over and kissed him on the mouth. When she pulled away, she saw through his act.

"You're really scared," she said, studying his face. "Aren't you?"

His eyes went wide for just a second before returning to their normal size. "No, I was just making a joke." He let out a nervous laugh. "I thought it would be—"

"It's okay if you are," she said, giving him a sympathetic smile. "Lots of people are afraid of heights."

"I'm not afraid of heights," he said, lowering his eyes. "I'm afraid of falling and hitting the ground."

"I'd be afraid, too, if we were in any *real* danger," she said, shifting in her seat to look down at the carnival. "Look at all the rides and games. I can see everything from up here."

Richie looked out, but not straight down like Madison. Just watching her grip the side of the cart and hang her head over made Richie feel nauseated. "I'll take your word for it," he said.

The Ferris wheel started to move again. Madison was still looking down at the carnival when she said, "What do you want to ride next?"

Richie was silent.

Madison spun around in her seat, making the cart sway back and forth. "Earth to Richie. You copy?"

"I'm thinking," Richie said, trying not to look frightened as the cart swayed. "How about a funhouse or something?"

"I saw three funhouses, but they're on the far side of the carnival. Probably best to save those for last."

As they made it all the way around, Richie got himself ready to exit the cart.

"What are you doing?" Madison said.

"We went around. Aren't we getting off now? Richie asked with a furrowed brow.

"Have you ever ridden the Ferris wheel before?"

"Just once. When I was a kid."

"Then you should know they normally have you go around more than one time."

Richie's face fell. The carny working the ride sent them around three more times. By the third time around, Richie had become slightly less afraid. He still wanted the hell off, but he felt better about not falling to his death.

When they got off the Ferris wheel, Madison took Richie by the hand, laced her fingers through his and led him to the next ride. They rode the Tilt-A-Whirl next to prepare themselves for the several other rides that would spin you around until you couldn't walk straight. They got those out of the way before purchasing some fried dough on a paper plate.

"Nutritious," Richie said after taking a bite. "I can almost feel my arteries clogging."

Madison chuckled and took a small piece off the plate. "Come on. There's still a lot we haven't gotten to yet."

They played all the classic carnival games. Even though they knew better than half of them were rigged, they still had fun.

By the time they finished with the games, the sun had set completely. The carnival's neon lights were glowing all around them.

"What time do you think this place closes?" Madison asked.

"Not sure. Maybe—"

"'Bout a half hour," said a man walking by.

"What kind of carnival closes right as it's getting dark?" Madison asked.

The man stopped and turned around. He was bone-thin, maybe in his late forties, with a cigarette tucked behind one of his ears. "Oh," he grinned, revealing teeth that neither Madison nor Richie cared to see. "We 'ave our reasons. Better jus' leave it at that."

The man chuckled to himself as he ambled away. When he was out of earshot, Richie said, "Come on."

"Where are we going?" she asked.

"To find that man a toothbrush," Richie said, then in the man's voice, "Better jus' leave it at that."

Madison placed her hand over her mouth to keep the laughter from bursting out. "Where to next?"

"We should head to the other side of the carnival and check out what we can before the place closes."

"We better hurry, then."

They walked quickly to the other side. Once there they found the bumper cars, which they couldn't pass up. After that ride, they strolled farther down and saw three funhouses, all of them with different themes and sizes. They started with the one closest to them. It was candy themed and just your run-of-the-mill funhouse: gravity-powered tipping floors, air jets that would go off randomly, and a revolving tunnel at the exit.

The second one was painted lime green and a lot smaller than the first one. Richie and Madison could tell right away that this one was designed for kids.

Madison checked her watch again. "If that guy was telling the truth, the carnival closes in about five minutes. Let's skip this one."

"Sounds good to m—" Richie stopped when he saw the front entrance of the last funhouse. There was only one thing that horrified Richie more than heights: clowns. The funhouse was black with red drippy lettering that said *The Clown House*. The front entrance was a fourteen-feet-tall clown head with a stretched-open mouth to allow you in.

"Whoa," Madison said, her eyes locked on the giant clown head. "This one looks intense."

Richie stayed silent.

"Richie?"

He blinked a few times, snapping out of it. "Yeah?"

"Are you okay?"

"Yeah. Why do you ask?"

"Your hands."

Richie looked down at his clenched fists. His knuckles had turned almost as white as his face.

"Don't tell me you're afraid of clowns too," she said with raised eyebrows.

Not afraid, Richie thought. *Terrified.*

"It's a carnival," she said, grinning. "Did you not think there'd be clo—"

"I'm not afraid of clowns," Richie said. He didn't sound convincing, not even to himself.

"They just gross me out."

Madison would have bought it, maybe, if not for his complexion turning a few shades lighter at the sight of the giant clown head. "Okay," she sighed. "The place closes soon anyway. Let's just leave."

Richie could tell she was disappointed, but he had an idea.

After a deep breath, he started laughing and holding his gut.

"What's so funny?" Madison asked.

"Do you think I'm *really* afraid of clowns? It was joke!"

She studied him for a few seconds, then started to laugh herself. "Thank goodness. I was starting to think I was dating a wuss."

Wuss. Ouch.

Truth was Richie did hate clowns, but he was going to tough it out for Madison. He heard the excitement in her voice when she said that the funhouse looked "intense." He'd be damned if they left without going in it.

As they walked up to the funhouse, Richie realized he had been so fixated on the giant clown head that he didn't see the carny manning the entrance; it was the skinny guy they had seen earlier that told them the park was closing soon. He was leaning up against the funhouse, his bony hands cupped in front of his mouth, about to light up a cigarette. When he saw Richie and Madison walking up, he stopped and parked the little bad habit back behind his ear.

"You two are 'bout a hair past a freckle too late," the carny said.

Madison checked her watch and raised it to show him. "We have three minutes before the place closes."

"Ah," the carny said as he raised a finger. "Right you are, missy, but I close this funhouse down early for a reason."

"Why?" she asked, her hands on her hips now.

"Damn place is haunted, that's why," he said, smirking. "I've been runnin' this funhouse for p'raps eighteen or nineteen years now. Hell, I'd guess that's prob'ly as long you two have been alive."

"I'm not buying it," Madison said, giving him a cold stare.

"Don't matter if you do or don't. She been in there a long time. Only had one person go in there and not make it back out. Well, two if you count her."

"Her?" Richie said. "What are you talking about?"

"A clown murdered a lady in there long ago. He liked her. She didn't feel the same way. Guy was a nut and couldn't let anyone else have her either, I reckon. Now, I'm doin' you kiddos a favor by shuttin' it down when it gets dark out. That's when she wakes up. During the day, she don't mess with nobody."

Madison rolled her eyes, clearly not believing a word the man said, and took Richie by the hand. "We'll be fine. Won't we, Richie?"

Richie nodded as he looked at the giant clown again. "Yeah," he said, shifting his eyes to the man. "We'll be fine."

A yellow-toothed grin spread across the carny's face. He saw Richie's fear of clowns all over his face. He'd seen that look a thousand times over the years working the funhouse. "That clown," he said, looking Richie in the eyes. "He'd be the least of your worries if you go in there."

Richie handed the tickets to him. "We'll take our chances."

The carny's grin faltered. "I still can't let you go in," he said, lowering his eyes and scratching his head. "If you two disappear in there, the cops are goin' to come—"

He looked back up just in time to see Madison and Richie go through the Clown's mouth.

"Oh, boy," he said, grabbing the cigarette from behind his ear. "This ain't good."

It was dark inside. Richie led the way through the funhouse. There were clowns everywhere, of course, which caused Richie's heart to beat about as fast as the flashing strobe lights. At some point, Richie looked back at Madison. She had a huge smile on her face.

"This funhouse is great, isn't it?" she asked.

"Totally," Richie said, walking through it at a brisk pace.

"Slow down a little. I want to see everything."

Richie slowed down, but he didn't really want to. Between the clowns, strobe lights, and mechanical clanking of moving floors, he was ready to find the exit.

"Check it out," Madison said, pointing ahead at a room with red lighting. The ceiling's light fixtures were hanging by wires. They'd go down a few feet and rise back up to the ceiling every few seconds. "How weird is that?"

Richie watched as the light fixtures went up and down. There were five of them, and under each red bulb was a circular section of the floor that would spin you around slowly. Richie was first to enter the room in the funhouse. He saw a myriad of photographs pinned to the walls, all of them of different clowns. He stepped on the first circular section and quickly went to the next one.

"This room is creepy," Madison said, as she spun around on the first circular section, looking at the photographs surrounding them.

"Couldn't agree more," Richie said, already at the other side of the room.

Madison stepped on the next section of moving floor, looking up at the light fixtures as they went up and down with a big smile on her face. Then her brow furrowed.

"Did you see that?" she asked Richie.

"See what?"

She was looking at the little six-inch hole in the ceiling where the wires were hanging.

The light bulb attached to the fixture ascended quicker this time. Instead of stopping when it reached the ceiling, it kept going. There was only an open hole now. When Madison saw what was looking down at her from the hole in the ceiling, her eyes went wide with terror.

"Madison," Richie said, watching her spin slowly as she looked up. "What are you doing?"

The ghost pressed her face up against the hole, locking eyes with Madison. Madison couldn't talk, couldn't even move. She just stood there, looking up as if in a trance. It wasn't until the ghost's arm shot out of the hole that she snapped out of it. She screamed just before the ghost's hand grabbed her by the throat, feeling her feet leave the ground as she was lifted in the air. Although, before Madison's face connected with the ceiling, she felt two hands wrap around her ankle.

Richie was pulling down as hard as he could, but the ghost wouldn't let go. Even with the red lighting, he saw his girlfriend's face turning a deep purple. Richie's grip on Madison's ankle was beginning to slip, then the lights in the funhouse went out. Suddenly, the smell of cigarette smoke permeated the air in the room. Two seconds later, the lights were back on. This time they were bright white lights instead of red. Richie saw the ghost release Madison and readied himself to catch her. In Richie's arms, Madison sucked in a deep breath as her trembling fingers touched her throat.

"You kids all right?"

Madison and Richie recognized the voice.

"What the hell was that?" Madison asked.

"Told you the place was haunted. That's why I wasn't goin' to let you two in," the carny said, then took a drag off the cigarette.

"We thought you were kidding," Richie almost yelled.

The carny grinned. "These bright lights will only keep her away for so long." The grin disappeared when he heard a thud from somewhere in the funhouse. "Y'all might want to skedaddle."

Richie and Madison made a beeline for the exit and didn't stop running until they got back to their car in the parking lot.

The carny was standing near the exit of the funhouse when he noticed his cigarette was almost down to the filter. He looked out at the carnival rides all around him and inhaled deeply.

When he exhaled the entire carnival went dark.

"How in the he—"

As his feet came out from underneath him, his head bounced off the metal platform hard enough to knock out a professional boxer. He was still barely conscious somehow, though. Just enough to realize that the ghost was pulling him back into the funhouse.

THE SMELL

LINDA HUDSON HOAGLAND

Jerry tended to drift into whatever jobs were available that would pay the rent. That attitude or lack of motivation was what led him into the mess he had stepped into with both feet planted, and the muck was rising to knee level.

He had been hired by a new neighbor to help clean out a house the neighbor had inherited from his uncle. There was also a garage and a couple of out buildings, so the job was going to take more than one day. He was being paid ten dollars an hour, which was more than he would earn at the local chicken or hamburger joint.

"When do we start?" he asked the new neighbor, Martin Stone.

"Tomorrow at 8:00 AM sharp," replied Stone with a smile.

Jerry walked back to the house he shared with his mother, a divorcee, and a longtime resident of Stillwell.

* * *

At 8:00 AM Jerry was knocking at Martin Stone's front door. There was a pause before Jerry knocked again a little bit louder.

"Okay, okay, go wait for me out back. I'll be there in just a couple of minutes," Stone shouted through the large, wooden door.

"Sure, sure," said Jerry as he turned to walk down the steps and proceeded to make his way around the house. Jerry glanced at each window as he walked. If the blinds were open he would take a peek inside. He had to shade his eyes with both hands to chase away the glare of the blinding morning sun.

He had always wanted to be invited inside the house so he could inspect the former neighbor's belongings. That had never happened.

Old Man Jonas Teague was a recluse who allowed no one into his house. The only time Jerry could remember a stranger entering through the front door was when the police broke it down to do a wellness check. Someone had reported the rank smell emanating from the surrounds of his property.

Jerry wasn't sure who reported it to the police, but he did remember the smell. Old Man Jonas had been dead for several days before the body was discovered and removed.

He wondered if the smell had completely left the house. He didn't smell it any longer outside, but that was a wide open space, not the confined area of a house.

Jerry was standing out back kicking at the dirt when Martin Stone opened the back door.

"I've got the key here. I'll toss it to you and you can open that padlock on the front door of the out building," Martin Stone said as he tossed the keys to Jerry's waiting hands.

The out building was actually three out buildings positioned so close to each other, train-style, that all three building could be accessed through a single front door.

Old Man Jonas must have cut a hole in the back wall of the first building directly in front of the door of the next out building so it would be a straight walk through, and he did the same thing to connect the third out building. A wooden walkway connected each building, and a roof had been constructed to make them all appear as one extra, extra, long out building. Old Man Jonas must have put a lot of time into doing all of that work.

Jerry opened the lock and stuck his head inside the first of the three connected buildings. He waited a few seconds as his eyes adjusted to the darkness before he stepped inside of the structure. He wasn't sure what he was going to run into if he blundered ahead.

Stone had not joined him yet, so he proceeded to check out the contents of the first section.

"Junk everywhere," he said with disgust as he shook his head. He picked up a couple of pieces of what looked like lawnmower parts. He dropped them back into the wooden box in which they had been placed awaiting disposal.

He moved into the second section where he saw more junk, but it was a bit cleaner and possibly much more useful. The good tools were stored in the second section along with some unopened packages for plumbing parts and other items that he unsure of how to use.

The third section surprised him. It was filled with flat screen televisions and other new electronic items.

He turned to walk back into the second section when Martin Stone appeared in front of him.

"Those are all mine, Jerry. I brought them here for storage. I have a mail order business, or I should say an email business, and I'm getting these items ready for shipment to customers," Stone explained.

"Sure, okay, what is your website and I'll check it out?" Jerry asked.

"I'll give it to you later. In the meantime, I want you to start in the first section and box up what is laying loose so it can be thrown out," said Stone.

Jerry walked to the first section of the out building and started tossing many unidentifiable items into boxes to be hauled away for disposal.

Martin Stone walked up behind Jerry and said in a loud voice, "I'll be back in an hour. I'll show you what you need to do next when I get back."

Jerry jumped back at the loud voice, almost bumping into Stone. It frightened him that Martin Stone would be sneaking up behind him like that.

Stone laughed, turned, and walked away from the out building towards the house.

Jerry heard a car engine roar to life and when he checked to see who it was, Stone backed out of the driveway.

Jerry immediately walked away from the out building and decided to check the back door of the house. He wanted to see if the door was unlocked so he could take a look inside without Martin Stone's presence.

The door was slightly ajar.

"Good, I finally get to see what's inside this place," Jerry said as he nudged the door a bit further so he could enter what looked like a kitchen.

A chill went through him as soon as he walked into the house. He glanced around warily. Something didn't seem right other than the fact that he was snooping around where he didn't belong and wasn't invited. He took a couple of steps toward what looked like the dining room.

Again, the chill raced through his body.

He heard a noise and turned his body towards the sound. Then he got a whiff of the smell.

"Hello? Is anyone there?" he asked in a weak whisper.

He didn't dare go any further until he figured out who or what made that noise. Instead, he turned tail and ran to the back door, leaving it ajar just as he had found it, and headed back to the out building to do his job.

"The spirit of Old Man Jonas must still be in that house," he mumbled as he gathered junk into boxes.

Martin Stone returned as he said, except that he was no longer driving a car. He was backing up a pickup truck into the space near the front door of the outbuilding.

"Help me load these boxes onto the truck bed and then you can quit for the day. I'll pay you for the full eight hours for today but I want you back here at 8:00 tomorrow," said Martin Stone as he pulled a wad of cash from his pocket and peeled off four twenty dollar bills, handing them to Jerry. Stone grabbed some of the boxes and helped load them onto the truck.

"Okay," said a puzzled Jerry. "Oh, before I leave could I ask you a question?"

"What?" asked Stone.

"Were you related to Old Man Jonas Teague?"

"Yes, he was my uncle. Why do you ask?"

"Nothing in particular. Just curious," said Jerry as he loaded the last box.

"I'm taking this load to the dump. I'll see you tomorrow," said Stone as Jerry turned to leave.

The short walk to his own house gave Jerry a few moments to ponder on what was happening.

The whole set-up looked odd. The inside of the house had not been tidied up and it still smelled of death. The out building that held new pieces of electronic items was definitely out of place. Jerry could see no reason to store those items in the out building for resale. That should have been stored in a secure place, such as inside the house.

"Mom, I don't think I'm going to go back to work for Martin Stone," he said when he got a chance to speak to her without any distractions.

"Why not? You need to work so you can have some spending money. It takes everything I make to keep a roof over our heads and food in our mouths," she said firmly.

"I know. I'll try to find something better, but I just don't like what's going on over there. Actually, I think what he is doing is illegal. I have no proof, but my heart tells me I shouldn't go back. It's not the work. I can do hard work, you know that. I just don't trust Martin Stone," he explained.

"Okay, Jerry. If you feel that strongly about it, go ahead and quit. I trust your instincts," said his mom with a comforting smile appearing on her lips.

* * *

Bright and early the next morning, Jerry did not show up to work. Martin Stone was pacing the ground looking at his watch, awaiting Jerry's arrival, while Jerry watched him from his own kitchen window.

"Aren't you going to tell him that you quit?" asked his mother.

"No, if I'm not there, he will get the message," Jerry said sheepishly.

As they stood gazing outside, some dark-clad, gun-toting men stealthily walked passed the window aiming those guns toward the out building in the neighbor's back yard.

There was a sudden burst of gunfire and loud shouts of "Drop the gun, now! Drop the gun, now!"

"Get back from the window, Jerry. You might be shot at by someone," whispered his mom.

"I told you I thought there was something illegal going on over there. Now, I have proof," Jerry said with a smile.

After many hours, days, months of investigation, and trial preparation, Jerry was asked to appear as a witness for the prosecution against Martin Stone.

The portion of the case against Martin Stone was mostly about the storage of stolen property. Of course, Jerry couldn't say it was stolen because he didn't know for sure. All he could testify to was that there were new items stored in that building.

The rest of the story encompassed the death of Old Man Jonas. It seemed that Martin Stone, his own nephew, had a hand in the death of Old Man Jonas.

Jerry was so glad he heeded the warning of trouble his heart had issued.

ABOUT THE AUTHORS

Lori C. Byington lives in Bristol, Tennessee with her husband, son, and two dogs. She is a Professor of Composition at King University in Bristol, TN, a graduate of King College (1985) and ETSU (1987), and her short stories have been published in several previous anthologies from Jan-Carol Publishing, Inc.

Bev Freeman resides in Unicoi County in the foothills of the Appalachian Mountains. Author of the mystery trilogy *The Madison McKenzie Files*, Bev's fourth mystery novel is in the works with the hope of completion in winter of 2022. Short ghost stories are her main focus recently, and her book *Haunts I've Known* is coming soon.

Jeff Geiger Jr. lives in Zephyrhills, Florida with his son. He is the author of *The White Room*, a suspense novel published in 2021. He has had short stories featured in *These Haunted Hills: A Collection of Short Stories Book 2 & Book 3*. You can find Jeff on Facebook: JeffGeigerJr, and on Instagram @jeffgeigerjr.

Linda Hudson Hoagland from Tazewell, Virginia, has written many mystery novels along with works of nonfiction, four collections of short writings, and four volumes of poems. Mysteries and short stories are her favorite pastime and she has won many awards as well as being published.

Jan Howery, a native of Southwest Virginia, writes with an Appalachian influence. Her many writings include "The Daisy Flower Garden," featured in the anthology *Broken Petals*, and "The Devil Behind the Barn" featured in the anthology *These Haunted Hills: A Collection of Short Stories*, "The Straight Back Chair," in *These Haunted Hills Book 2*, "Right or Wrong," featured in *Wild Daisies*, "The Love of Daisies" in *Scattered Flowers*, and "Dreams of Being a Teacher" in *Daffodil Dreams*. Other writings include fashion and health columns for the Appalachian regional magazine for women, *Voice Magazine for Women*.

Pauline Petsel's very unusual life experiences began after the births of her three children. She began her work as an author after being told she needed to write a book because no one would ever believe so much could happen to one person. Pauline and her husband moved to Tennessee about sixteen years ago and she has been writing books ever since. Two years ago her beloved husband of sixty years, passed away. Her books are now her life.

Courtnee Turner Hoyle resides in her own house of secrets with her children and husband. After obtaining a graduate degree, she spent years avoiding sweet tea, chocolate, and unannounced visitors. Hoyle's books, *My Brother's Keeper*, *Finding Emma*, and *Rasputin's Scorn*, have won gold awards. Hoyle works as an editor and travel agent, and can be found on Instagram (pale_woods_mysteries), Facebook, and TikTok. She enjoys reading, writing, and visiting strange and unusual places all over the world.

81

ALSO BY JAN-CAROL PUBLISHING:

These Haunted Hills
These Haunted Hills Book 2
These Haunted Hills Book 3

Jan-Carol
Publishing, Inc

"every story needs a book"

LITTLE CREEK BOOKS
MOUNTAIN GIRL PRESS
EXPRESS EDITIONS
ROSEHEART
BROKEN CROW RIDGE
FIERY NIGHT
HEIRLOOM EDITIONS
SKIPPY CREEK

www.JANCAROLPUBLISHING.com